THE SEASON OF *Secrets*

Q.B. TYLER

Content Editing: Kristen Portillo—Your Editing Lounge
Cover Design: Emily Witting Designs
Interior Formatting: Stacey Blake—Champagne Book Design

For everyone that was asking for Wes' book from the moment you met him in *The Worst Kept Secret*.

Happy Holidays, babes!

Halfway through writing *The Worst Kept Secret,* I decided to write Wes and Raegan's story and give it a little holiday twist because I wanted to write a steamy hookup between a billionaire and his assistant (that he's been in love with since she started, because obviously) after their office holiday party. (Also, this book was supposed to be a cute short novella and somehow doubled in length by the end.)

It is important to note that *The Season of Secrets* serves as a prequel to *The Worst Kept Secret.* This book takes place a year and a half before Theo and Avery's story. While you will see them in this, they are *not* together yet! So just to make sure you're clear on the timeline:
The Worst Kept Secret begins in May 2023 and this book begins in December 2021.

If you haven't read *The Worst Kept Secret* yet, that's fine too! You can read about Raegan and Wes now, and *then* if you want more of the Graham family you can move on to Raegan's dad and the girl that lives next door! (*And more Wes and Raegan!*)

Enjoy!

Xoxo

THE SEASON OF *Secrets*

Prologue

Raegan

"SO, WHAT TIME ARE YOU COMING OVER TONIGHT?" I hear from the other side of the cubicle I share with Marissa Collins my mentor turned work best friend at Beckham Securities. I spin around in my chair and meet her gaze as she bites into a granola bar.

"Maybe seven?" I shift in my chair, pull my pencil skirt down, and cross my legs. "The party starts at eight, right?"

She nods and stands up to move closer to me. "I can't wait for you to experience your first holiday party here." She whistles and lets out a laugh. "It's…something."

Marissa is a year older than me but has been working for the company for almost three years and while I was assigned to her to learn the ropes six months ago when I started, she's also taken it upon herself to give me all the inside gossip, and more importantly, what men to stay away from, what women aren't *girls' girls*, and the best places to go for lunch. From the beginning, she always invited me to happy hours with her friends and did her best to make me feel included. I've only been here about six months, since I graduated college, and I've thoroughly enjoyed my *first job* experience.

"Well, don't scare her," a familiar voice interrupts and then I see Liam, a guy from sales that Marissa is convinced has a crush on me. He's standing at the entrance to our cubicle, dressed in jeans and a polo because it's *casual Friday.* "It's fun but it's not too crazy."

"She's six months post-grad from a party school; she thrives on crazy." Marissa giggles and I glare at her comment about Penn State. *Okay, yes it may be a party school, but I still graduated Summa Cum Laude which meant I spent more time studying than partying.*

Okay, half and half.

"It's definitely a good time," Liam adds and gives me a smile followed by a wink. "You coming to Marissa's early?"

"That's the plan." I nod and give him a smile. I'm not interested in Liam despite his boyish good looks and southern charm, but I'm nothing if not polite.

"Great, I'll see you tonight then." He grins, revealing perfectly straight teeth. "Do you want—" he starts when another voice cuts through our conversation.

"Mr. Patterson." I freeze, hearing my boss's deep sultry voice as he appears next to Liam at the entrance to my cubicle, taking up more space than Liam does. He's so…*big and really just overpowering. Not to mention, gorgeous.* He has black frames that sit in front of blue eyes and a tattoo that always peeks out under the cuff of his jacket making me wonder if he's got a sleeve. His hair is sandy brown but peppered with gray making me think he'll be a *silver fox* in a few years. "Miss Graham, Miss Collins." He nods at us and I know my cheeks have to be pink at the thought of being reprimanded. My hands twist in my lap nervously when his eyes linger on me a moment longer than they did on Marissa's.

"Mr. Beckham," Liam says with a nod. "We were just talking about the holiday party."

"You're a long way from your desk," Mr. Beckham responds and I wince, hoping Liam is not about to get in trouble.

"Well, I'm actually on my way out for an appointment, and thought I would drop by to talk to them about tonight," he explains. "We are meeting up before the holiday party."

"I see." Mr. Beckham looks Liam up and down and narrows his gaze. "Without your coat or your things?" He raises an eyebrow and slaps his back before moving down the hall towards his office. "Flirt on your own time, Patterson," he calls over his shoulder.

Liam glares after him before turning back to Marissa. "God, he's such a dick."

Marissa fixes her headband keeping her jet-black curls back and points at me. "To everyone but Raegan."

Liam frowns and turns to me, eyeing me curiously. "Is that so?"

My eyebrows pinch as I turn to look at her. "Marissa, he's not exactly friendly towards me either."

"No, but he's not a hard ass to you like he is to everyone else."

"He's not a hard ass to you!" I argue.

"He used to be. The only reason he's lightened up now is because I'm friends with *you*." She wiggles her eyebrows up and down. "I've been here three years, and I've never seen him respond to anyone the way he responds to you. He's so nice to you! Remember that time he brought you coffee?"

"He didn't *bring* me coffee! I accidentally left my coffee in the copy room and he brought it!" I glower at her. This is how rumors start and being the newest and thereby the lowest on the totem pole, that's the last thing I need being spread about me.

"Wes Beckham hasn't been in the copy room in years, and the second you set foot in there, suddenly, he knows where the fuck it is." Marissa rolls her eyes and turns back to her computer. "Liam…" she waves her hand towards him, "go before you get in trouble."

I watch him leave before I roll my chair closer to hers so I can whisper. "What are you saying exactly?"

She turns her head towards me and raises an eyebrow making me wonder if she can see the hope written all over my face. She blinks her dark brown eyes rapidly. "That the boss is into you."

"Oh." I let out a breath because, *fuck what does that even mean?*

"But there's a million fraternization policies in place, so he won't make a move."

"Of course not." I shake my head and stare at her computer screen because I'm too nervous to meet her gaze.

"Oh em gee!" she says and grabs my face to turn it toward her. "Do you have a crush on Mr. Beckham?"

"No! No no no," I protest, probably too much because she gives me a look that tells me that she's not buying what I'm selling.

"Oh my God. Okay, look," she turns her chair to face me and puts her hands on my shoulders, "Wes is a huge football fan, just arrange for your ex-NFL player hot dad to meet him and you'll be in!" She taps my nose and I scrunch it in response.

"Can you not?" I groan, hearing yet another woman in my life refer to my father as *hot.*

"Oh, I love this, you guys could like—do it in his office. He could have *you* for lunch if you know what I mean." She raises her eyebrows mischievously.

"No, whatever do you mean?" I ask sarcastically as I roll back to my desk.

"That he'd eat you out," she says, and I spin around to meet her amused expression.

"Marissa!" I whisper shout and she giggles as she hops out of her chair and slides her sweater on.

"I'm going to get a coffee. You want anything?"

"I'm good, thanks." I narrow my eyes at her and peek my head outside the cubicle as she leaves. *What if someone heard that?* The sound of the phone ringing makes me jump and I've already convinced myself that it's Human Resources calling me to their office to discuss appropriate office talk.

Shit. I think when I see the familiar extension on my phone.

"He didn't hear anything." I snort, shaking my head. *Marissa wasn't that loud.* "Hi, Mr. Beckham." I catch myself twirling my finger around the chord like some lovesick teenager getting a call from their crush. *Get a grip!*

"Miss Graham, can you come to my office please?" I wonder if he can hear my heart pounding in my chest.

Relax, he probably just needs something.

"Of course, be right there." I hang up the phone and quickly pull out my compact to check my lipstick and my hair before I head down the hall to his office.

I knock on his door and when I hear his voice telling me to come in I take a deep breath before I push inside. His office is huge. Floor to ceiling windows line two of the four walls giving the perfect view of the Philadelphia skyline. I've been in here a few times at dusk and the way the sun sets over the city is gorgeous turning the whole room into a sensual amber color.

He's sitting at his desk staring at his computer but as soon as I enter the office, his eyes rise to meet mine. They sweep over me once like he's cataloging what I'm wearing and I suddenly feel like my skirt may be too short. *No, it's just above my knees!*

I am rarely nervous around people; my father taught me to be confident and well-spoken. Yet something about Wes Beckham makes me feel anything but those things. I feel like a silly girl who has a crush on an older man that she can't have.

His eyes move to mine and I see a smile pulling at his lips. "I just wanted to make sure you saw the itinerary for next week."

There is a team of us flying to Miami for a few days for a new project, and while Mr. Beckham usually doesn't go, it's one of his biggest clients and he wants to make sure everything runs smoothly. Being his assistant means I'm going as well.

"Yes." I nod. "I confirmed everything. We are all set to leave on Thursday."

He nods and turns back to his screen. "I've decided I'm going to head down a day earlier than everyone, so can you ensure the jet will be ready on Wednesday?"

"Of course." I nod, clasping my hands in front of me. He doesn't say anything else and I suddenly feel awkward, like I should say something. "Was there anything else?" I swallow, and when his eyes turn back to me, my skin starts to tingle under his gaze. I'm wearing four-inch heels and I suddenly feel like I'm a baby deer trying to stand for the first time, unable to keep my balance in them. My eyes dart around the room, trying to avoid his gaze.

"You are welcome to stay and fly down with everyone or you can come with me early." My eyes dart back to his and I note he's turned away from his computer screen to face me head on.

Alone on a jet with him?

Well, not alone, there will be a pilot and at least one flight attendant, obviously.

"Well, as your assistant, I would assume I should fly down with you?"

He nods, giving me a polite smile. "Very well. Make sure you add an additional room at the hotel for the extra night."

Am I…sweating? Jesus Christ, get me the fuck out of here before I completely embarrass myself.

I turn around to leave when I hear his voice again. "Miss Graham?"

Fuck.

"Yes?" I turn around.

"I'm not sure what you've been told about the office holiday party…" He trails off. "But don't let anyone convince you to do anything you don't want to do." He lowers his gaze and I almost feel like he's…warning me?

My eyebrows pinch slowly and I cock my head to the side. "Is this you telling me to make good choices tonight?" The words fly out of my mouth before I can stop them and while I hadn't meant for them to sound flirty, I hear the cheeky undertone and hope he just takes it as a joke.

I rarely see him smile and I know he has dimples, but now when he flashes a grin at me, I'm speechless at how gorgeous he looks. "Something like that."

I swallow, trying not to let out the breath my lungs are dying for as the tension mounts between us. "Well, I got it, no need to worry. I'll be good," I promise.

He narrows his eyes. "I just know that you're one of the youngest people here and also one of the newest so I wouldn't want you to get caught up in anything. Every year, there's always a group hauled into HR on Monday."

I nod, not knowing what to say that wouldn't be flirty or cheeky or sarcastic. "Okay, well, I'll see you tonight then."

"You're not planning to drive, are you?" He asks and I briefly wonder if everyone is getting this inquisition.

I cock my head to the side, curiously. "I have to ask, are you *this* invested in all of your employees'...well-being?"

His eyes widen, like he's surprised I questioned him versus answering him and he turns back to his computer. "It's my company. Thereby, I do feel responsible in some ways for what happens there and once you all leave. While you're all adults, there's a number that don't act like it after a few drinks."

"I see, well I planned to Uber, so no worries," I assure him.

"Good." He doesn't look at me as he picks up his phone and holds it to his ear. "You can go now."

I don't speak another word before I'm out the door, and finally, I can breathe.

Chapter ONE

Raegan

I TURN IN THE MIRROR FOR THE HUNDREDTH TIME BEFORE pulling off the green velvet dress that I planned to wear weeks ago that suddenly doesn't feel right. I then try on the burgundy off-the-shoulder jumpsuit *for the second time,* before I huff in frustration, realizing that I don't want to wear pants. I whine and let out an aggravated sigh as I watch the time inch closer to six, when I still have to curl my hair.

"You good in there?" I hear from the other side of the door.

I pull on a robe and open the door to reveal my dad standing on the other side. "I don't have anything to wear."

He lowers his gaze and lifts an eyebrow at me. "What did I tell you about that phrase?"

"That you don't want to hear it." I imitate him. "But I don't!" I turn towards my room and the tornado that hit it looking at the clothes strewn everywhere.

"Your closet is bigger than mine and packed to the brim, you have something to wear Raegan."

"Not to my first office party! It's not like I can wear any of my college party clothes. I'm already the youngest person there, I'm trying to look more mature."

My dad sighs and shakes his head like he's not prepared to listen to my *I hate all my clothes* spiel. "Alright, well. Good luck. What time should I expect you home?"

I scrunch my nose. "Do I suddenly have a curfew?"

"No, but excuse me for wanting to make sure you get home safe?" He crosses his arms over his chest. "Or are you staying at your friend's house?"

"No. I'll be home later, but I don't know. They said the office party can get a little out of hand. So, it could be ten, could be four…" I shrug.

He chuckles and rolls his eyes. "Keep me posted please and behave yourself. You don't want to get the reputation as someone who doesn't know how to handle their alcohol and has to be *watched* at office parties. Every company has a couple." I nod, remembering Mr. Beckham's warning. At least this one is coming from someone I'm used to getting lectures from.

"I got it, Dad."

"Alright." He looks behind me and then at me. "Don't you have a sparkly skirt?"

I raise my eyebrows at the swift change in conversation. "A sparkly skirt? You mean like sequins?"

"Sure." He shrugs. "A lot of women wear those to holiday parties. Festive or whatever."

I gasp. "Oh! I do have a sparkly skirt!" I say clapping my hands. "And I can wear it with this black top?" I tap my chin.

"Okay, I'm not here to style you." He snorts as he begins to walk down the hall. "You've got it from here."

I close the door, a pang of sadness shooting through me that I can't call the one person who would know exactly what I should wear. *I mean I could call her,* but there was a ninety percent chance she wouldn't answer and a one hundred percent chance she'd call me back two days from now.

I stare at my phone for a moment, thinking about calling my mother before I decide on the next best person. I slide on the skirt and a black long-sleeved top that shows off a tasteful amount of cleavage and my favorite Jimmy Choo heels.

I press the button to Facetime Avery, the girl who lives next door and is the closest person I've had to a sister. It's her junior year of college, and while she went to school in state, she's still about forty minutes away and probably well on her way to being drunk for the night.

"Hello?" She holds her phone close to her face and whispers.

I frown, wondering why she's talking so quietly. "Why are you whispering?"

"Because I'm at the library, what's up!" She pulls the phone away and I see that she's not wearing a stitch of makeup and her curly hair is pulled into a messy bun. Her hazel eyes are slightly red and I briefly wonder if she's been sleeping. Avery is like my honorary little sister and I worry about her just like I do about my little brother Lucas.

"Oh, I figured you'd be out partying."

"Ugh," she scoffs. "I wish. I have my hardest final exam on Monday before I come home for winter break."

"Okay, well I won't keep you, but do I look okay?" I set my phone down and back up. "For my office holiday party?"

"Oooh yes! You look hot," she whispers with a thumbs up, "but still sophisticated."

"Thank you, that's what I was going for! You're the best." I clap my hands.

She giggles and blows me a kiss. "Have fun!"

"Good luck with your test and see you next week!" I wave before hanging up.

Thirty minutes later, I'm making my way downstairs after ordering an Uber to grab the bottle of tequila I bought to take to Marissa's house. Then, the thought hits me that maybe I should take something like champagne or wine and not something that could have people wanting to take their clothes off before we even get to the party.

"Dad! Can I take some of this champagne in here?" I call from his den, where he keeps all of his good liquor.

"Whatever you want, Rae!" He calls back.

I grab two bottles, leaving the tequila behind. I walk through our massive kitchen into the living room to find my dad seated on the couch flipping through the channels and it's times like this I wish he had a woman in his life. He doesn't do much but work and hang out with me and Lucas when we're free, but Lucas goes to college in New York and I usually go out once a weekend. I feel like he's probably lonely on those nights.

"Are you going out?" I ask, hoping he's planning to leave the house at some point.

"No." He shakes his head and sits up slightly. "Do you want me to drive you?"

"Yeah, that's great. I'll have my dad drop me off at a party." I laugh, because I know my dad would drive me in a heartbeat if I wanted him to. "I just wasn't sure if you had plans. You're just going to stay in?"

"Yes, Rae." He laughs. "My partying days are behind me."

"You don't have to party, you could go…to a bar and hang out?"

"I could." He chuckles. "I do not want to." He gets up and

makes his way towards me putting his hand on my shoulder and gives it a gentle squeeze. "You okay?"

"Yeah, I just...don't want you to be bored." *Or lonely during the holidays.* He's barely dated since he and my mother divorced and I feel like it has to be hard sometimes.

"Well, I appreciate the concern, hon, but I'm fine," he tells me with a smile. He wraps an arm around me and kisses my temple. "You look beautiful." He gives me a playful nudge. "Very sophisticated."

"That's what Avery said!" I look down at my phone to check the status of my Uber.

"You talked to Avery?" He asks.

"Yeah, I needed a woman's opinion." I look up from my phone just as he moves away from me towards the refrigerator.

"How's she doing?" He pulls out a beer.

"Great, she was studying," I tell him just as my phone beeps. "Oh, my Uber is here! Don't wait up!" I say over my shoulder.

"Be safe. Call me if you need me," he calls after me just before I shut the door behind me.

Marissa's pregame consists mostly of the people who work on our floor and a few people from other departments. *Beckham Securities* is headquartered in a twelve-story building with over four hundred employees taking up the top six floors, and it seems like there are at least thirty of us here at her townhouse.

"Oh yay, finally!" Marissa says as she pulls me through her entry and into her kitchen where people are talking and drinking casually. "You hungry?" She points to the finger foods she has out. Marissa really is the perfect hostess and whenever she has people over, she always has multiple charcuterie boards and themed appetizers and drinks. She hands me a glass of red wine with cranberries, apples, and rosemary sticking out of the top. "It's Christmas sangria!"

"I brought champagne?" I offer and she claps her hands.

"Oh lovely." She takes it from me and puts it in her fridge. "You really didn't need to bring anything though. Just your very cute self." She points at my outfit and gives me an impressed look. "You look great. I have to finish getting ready though. Make yourself at home," she says, talking a mile a minute before she dashes out of the kitchen and up the stairs. I want to tell her I'll go with her because I definitely feel more comfortable around my coworkers when she's there too. I take a sip of the sangria and cough immediately at the strength of it.

"Yeah, it's strong." Liam chuckles. "You know Marissa is a little heavy-handed."

"Did she use the entire bottle of bourbon?" I laugh as I put the glass down, reaching instead for a bottle of vodka to make myself a mixed drink where I can control the amount of alcohol that goes in.

"You look beautiful," Liam tells me. I tuck a dark wavy strand behind my ear and give him my best *I really just want to be friends* smile.

"Thank you! You look very dashing as well." Liam always dresses well, and I'll admit he looks really nice tonight wearing a white collared shirt under a gray cashmere sweater under a navy blazer making him look like he should be walking the runway for some designer winter fashion show. He taps his glass against mine as soon as I'm finished making it just as a girl that I vaguely recognize but can't remember her name approaches us.

"I thought you were coming right back," she says without so much as a glance in my direction.

"Morgan, you remember Raegan, right?" Liam points at me and I smile and give a small wave.

"Right, the new girl!" she says and I try to ignore the underlying condescension in her voice.

"Well, it's been six months, but...yeah!"

She plays with the ends of her pin-straight raven black hair, that's pulled high into a sleek ponytail. "How are you liking it?"

"I love it; everyone is really nice." I smile and she returns it with one that seems more fake than polite before turning back to Liam.

"We've been waiting for you to start the next round of quarters."

"Oh, start without me." He shrugs and I see the flash of hurt on Morgan's face before she looks at me and then nods. I don't think he meant to be dismissive, but I can feel the sting nonetheless.

"You should come play too," she says to me as an afterthought and I realize that she might have a little crush on Liam and thinks I'm the problem. I want to tell her that I'm not and more importantly, not interested in being more than friends. She walks away, back towards the living room leaving us alone, and I almost wish she would have pressed harder for him to join her.

"Do you want to play?" He asks and nods towards the living room.

"Actually, I'm going to go check on Marissa," I tell him. "I'll be right back," I say before moving up the stairs towards her room. I've only been up here a few times, so I hope it's okay that I just come up here. I knock on her bedroom door. "Hey, it's Raegan."

"Oh, come in!" I hear called from the other side.

I push through her door just to see her come out of her connecting bathroom curling her eyelashes. I note she's wearing a burgundy lace long-sleeved dress that comes just above her knees, making me grateful I changed so that we weren't wearing the same color. She's wearing a lipstick that is almost the same color and it looks gorgeous against her brown skin. "I'm almost ready! You okay?"

"It's just a little…overwhelming. I'm used to drinking with people I know. I'm an extrovert but to an extent. Plus, I'm sober."

"Drink more!" She tucks a hair behind her ear.

"I don't want to be sloppy drunk at our office party. Besides, it's only seven thirty!" I hold my drink up. "This is vodka."

"Oh good." She takes a long sip of her sangria before setting it down.

"I think you're right about Liam, by the way. How do I let him know I just want to be friends? Preferably before Morgan pushes me down a flight of stairs?"

"Ooh yeah." She winces as she begins to brush her mascara over her lashes. "Well, to be fair, Liam shouldn't have slept with her."

My eyes widen in shock as I mentally go over that interaction the three of us just had through a new lens. "He has?!"

"Mmmm. I want to say at one of our retreats? Or maybe one of the summer cookouts? Maybe both?"

"Oh no wonder she was looking at me like she hates me."

"Ignore her. I do feel bad that Liam leads her on, but aside from that she actually kind of sucks." Liam and Marissa are good friends so I wonder if she's also a bit jaded by whatever Liam has told her. She turns off the light in her bathroom before moving towards her closet to grab a pair of heels. "So…are you going to make a move on the boss man tonight?"

"What?!" I shake my head. "How much have you had to drink already?"

She shakes her head, refuting my claim that alcohol is the only reason for her statement. "Only like two of these. You totally should!"

"Why would I do that? Do you want me to get fired?"

She snorts. "First of all, if he went around firing every employee that's hit on him, he'd have no employees."

A spike of jealousy shoots through me. "Oh? So…you've hit on him?" I try to sound as relaxed as possible.

"Feeling territorial?" she asks with a smirk. "But no, he screamed at me on my first day, and then I spent the day crying in the bathroom after that so he really does nothing for my vagina." She rolls her eyes. "And I don't mean literally every employee obviously. I just mean women flirt with him all the time. You've got eyes. I'm sure you can see why."

I do remember her telling me when I started that nothing could be worse than her first day, but I never realized it was because he yelled at her. I find myself getting irritated at his lack of sensitivity. *On her first day? Rude.* "Well, I'm not going to hit on him. Besides, he's like my dad's age," I explain. I've never been attracted to an older man, and I'll admit this attraction to Mr. Beckham feels…different yet *hot.*

"So? A little daddy kink never hurt anyone."

A flash of going over his knee as he spanks me comes out of nowhere and knocks me a little off kilter. I shift my weight, trying my best to squeeze my thighs together as I imagine saying that *D* word while his lips explore my body.

"Uh huh." My eyes snap to Marissa's and see the look she's giving me. "That's what I thought."

It's almost nine before we all get to the party and it's definitely in full swing when we enter the huge hall that they rented out for the occasion. There are several Christmas trees of different sizes set up around the room, some decorated, and some covered in fake snow, and one large one positioned at the entrance to the party where a photographer is taking pictures. There is garland hanging in every archway with strings of white lights and gold and ivory ribbon wrapped around it. All of the standing tables are covered with a deep forest green tablecloth with holly and tiny lit candles on top. Everything looks so festive and the room smells like cinnamon and pine and a wave of sad nostalgia hits me.

Christmas is supposed to be a joyous time, but for me and my brother, it just reminds us of our parents splitting up. Most teenagers our age were getting their first cell phones for Christmas, but Lucas and I were getting the news that our mom was moving out and that we'd be enrolled in new schools the following year.

I can still remember hearing my dad asking her to wait until after Christmas to tell us she was moving out to give us one more holiday of normalcy, but she'd wanted to spend it with *him*. I scrunch my nose thinking about my stepfather who I've said maybe a hundred words total to him in the six years they've been married. My dad wasn't particularly upset that she was moving out from what I observed, but he was worried about me and my brother, and how every Christmas would now be associated with our parents splitting up. Even now, the Christmas season usually reminds me *at least once* that I cried myself to sleep the night of Christmas Eve. Not to mention, I think I can count on one hand the number of times I've actually seen my mother on Christmas Day since then.

"You okay? You kind of spaced out." Marissa stands in front of me with two glasses of champagne with cranberries floating inside of it. She hands it to me and I take a healthy sip, already feeling the buzz from the vodka I had at her house wearing off.

"Yeah, Christmas just brings back memories, that's all." My eyes pan the room and as they scan the table with the entire senior team—including my very delicious boss who I'd just had my first fantasy about—everything around me just seems to fade away. His eyes are already on me slowly dragging up my frame and when they meet mine, he smiles and nods like he likes what I'm wearing or he's happy I'm here. Either way, I relish in his unspoken praise.

"Oh my God, you so love him. How did I not realize this?!" When I turn my head to Marissa, she's staring at me. "Come, let's get some food."

I follow her whispering, "I don't love him, Marissa. Besides, there are no fraternization policies, remember?"

"So? Don't get caught!" She giggles as we make our way towards one of the massive tables lined with every food possible. "I caught that look he was giving you. He is unashamedly into you, Raegan."

I want to tell her about going on the Miami trip with him a day early, but I decide now is not the time. I take another sip of the champagne, hoping the bubbles will settle the butterflies floating around in my stomach brought on by Marissa saying he's into me.

"You wouldn't judge me?"

"Judge you for what?" she asks as she opens one of the trays.

"I mean…say I did…" I pan the room, my eyes searching for him before I turn back to her when I don't see him in the same spot. "You wouldn't judge me for hooking up with the boss? Don't people hate women like that? Will people think I'm just trying to sleep my way to the top?"

"First of all, no one is going to know. So no one will think that," she says as we continue to move through the line. "Here, the crab balls are bomb. The restaurant that usually caters our events is the best in the city!" She puts some on my plate. "Definitely get the lobster too."

"And second of all?" I press. "What about you?"

"Why would I judge you or think that? We're friends. Why wouldn't I want you to get some?" She giggles as we move through the rest of the line and move to a high-top table.

"I'm not saying it's going to happen," I tell her as I take a sip of my champagne.

A waiter walks by carrying a tray of more glasses and Marissa plucks two as he passes. "Thank you, sir! I'll take those."

She slides one across the table to me and I shoot her a glare. "I'm not done with this one!"

She rolls her eyes and downs her glass before picking up the fresh one. "I'm not buzzed and I need to be." She pops a piece of cheese in her mouth.

"Ladies," I hear from behind me and when I turn around, I see Mr. Beckham standing there holding a highball glass of what looks like the sangria from Marissa's pregame. "You both look lovely. Very festive," he says nodding at us both.

I look him over and give him a smile over my glass. "You do too. I like your tie." I point at his red tie that is peppered with silver snowflakes. It's the only pop of color amidst his black suit and white shirt.

"I thought about wearing a Santa suit but thought that may be a little over the top."

Marissa snorts into her drink and clears her throat. "Sorry."

I do my best not to glare at her before turning back to him. "Maybe a little bit." I don't know what to say, but I know I don't want him to leave even if we are just engaging in mindless small talk. "What are you drinking?" I point at his drink.

"Ah, one of the festive cocktails. A cranberry bourbon sour."

"Is it good?" *Be more lame, Raegan, PLEASE.*

"It's not bad," he holds out his glass towards me and my eyes widen at his implication. "Do you want to try it?"

Yes! Try it! He wants to share his drink with you! HOT. "No, that's okay." I chuckle. "I'm not really a bourbon drinker anyway."

"Ah, to be twenty-one again." He chuckles and I narrow my gaze at him.

"I'll be twenty-two next month, thank you very much." I giggle and he smiles, revealing that dimple again and I lock my knees to prevent them from buckling.

"Any big plans?"

"My dad usually takes my brother and I to Aspen to go skiing, but we haven't really talked about it this year."

"You ski?" he asks.

I nod. "I do ski. My parents had me and my brother on the slopes at a very young age."

"Well, on our next company winter retreat, I'll have to see your skills."

"Miss Graham, Miss Collins," I hear, and then I see Christopher Holt, the CFO for *Beckham Securities* who seems to be a close friend of Mr. Beckham. I know he's younger but I'm not sure by how much and while I don't think he's nearly as good looking as Mr. Beckham, he certainly is no stranger to female attention either. "Wes, can I steal you for a second?"

"Is it absolutely necessary?" He glares at Christopher and I turn my gaze to Marissa, so it doesn't seem like I'm trying to be nosy.

"It issss," he drawls before turning him away from our table.

"Okay, he was totally flirting!" Marissa says as soon as they're out of earshot.

I stare after them, watching as Christopher laughs about

something and slaps him on the back as they leave the room entirely. I frown, wondering where he's going before turning back to Marissa. "He offered you his drink! That joke about the Santa suit? It wasn't even funny. I laughed because he attempted to make a joke...to make *you* laugh. Oh, this is freaking good TV," she says. "Let's get you some hard liquor. The champagne isn't cutting it and you need to loosen up."

"I am loose!"

"No, but maybe some Grey Goose will help." She does a shimmy, referring to that familiar Fergie song and hands me my clutch as she drags me towards the bar. "And then the winter retreat thing? Rae, we don't even haaaave a winter retreat! He's probably going to create one just for an excuse to ski with you! I am watching your romance just *blossom* in front of me!" She giggles as we make it to the bar where she orders us each a vodka soda. "Make hers a double." She points at me.

"Marissa!" I protest.

She ignores me and hands me the glass, which I already know has way more vodka than soda and I scrunch my nose before I squeeze at least three limes in it.

Chapter TWO

WES

"YOU'RE LUCKY I GOT YOU OUT OF THERE WHEN I did. You wait until you've got the whole fucking office staring at you to choose to stare at your assistant like you want to rip her clothes off?" Chris says as we step onto the heated patio and he hands me a cigar. I shake my head as he lights his and puts it to his lips.

"Fuck." I groan as I take a long sip of my drink which isn't half bad for flavored whiskey. "Was it that obvious?"

"I don't know, everyone is starting to feel their drinks, so maybe no one noticed but I know you, and *I* could tell."

I rub my forehead. "I think Marissa could too." I lean against the railing and rub a hand through my hair. "She looks so goddamn gorgeous." I start towards the door to go back inside. "I have to talk to her again."

"Hold on there, Romeo." He puts a hand up, pushing it

against my chest to force me backward. "Not with a room full of people and you know Dana from HR doesn't even drink so she notices everything!"

"Relax, I'm not going to fuck her on top of a table. I'm just going to talk to her."

"You haven't talked to half the people in there and you're going to circle back to talk to our newest employee! You're being obvious and thinking with your dick."

"You think I don't know that? I don't even want to talk to half the people in there. I'm usually preparing my exit right around now and I'm still here." I run my fingers over my tie, remembering her compliment and I grin at Chris. "She said she liked my tie."

"Well, by all means, just propose to her now," he jokes.

I shoot him a glare and my middle finger. "Remind me of the rules again." I grunt even though I damn near have them memorized by the number of times I've read them searching for a loophole.

He rolls his eyes and lets out a sigh. "Policy dictates that a relationship between senior management and their direct reports are prohibited as well as employees that are separated by at least two levels in chains of command. You own the company, Wes. Everyone is off limits to you."

"Fuck me." I groan, hearing the very black and white rules that prohibit me from touching Raegan Graham.

"I'm pretty much the only person you can fuck without it being a problem, but it's going to be a no from me," he jokes and I give him a look letting him know I'm far from amused. "Look, I'm not saying don't do it. You know I've slept with a few women from the company, just make sure she knows the deal and that she's also into it and compliant so she doesn't slap you with a sexual harassment lawsuit." He scratches his stubbled jaw.

"Right."

"She has to make the move Beck, and you cannot *guide* her to the move," he says using his nickname for me.

Chris and I have been friends ever since college. I was a senior when he was a freshman and I was his mentor. I thought of him as the little brother I always wanted and we managed to stay friends amidst me graduating and moving to different states. When I decided to start a company, I knew no one else better equipped to be my CFO. I was barely off the phone with him before he was packing his bags to move to Philadelphia to help me set up. I trust him with everything, including the very intense crush I have on my twenty-one—*almost twenty-two*—year old assistant.

Fuck, I want her. I still remember the day she interviewed. She'd made it through two interviews with human resources and I was the final one. I'd been through four assistants that month and I was fucking tired of the incompetency, so I told them I would be interviewing this next one so I could assure they weren't a complete idiot.

I did not expect Raegan Graham to walk through the door.

Six Months Prior:

"Come in," I bark towards the door, dreading this interview, when the sexiest scent surrounds me and I hear the door shut.

"Hello, Mr. Beckham." Her voice is confident and doesn't waver, and when I turn my eyes toward the sound, all of the air leaves my lungs when I see the most stunning woman I've ever seen in my life. Blue eyes the color of the ocean and dark brown hair, almost black that hangs around her shoulders in curls except for a few pieces she has pulled back out of her face. Despite the fact that she's wearing a pants suit, I'm already picturing what her legs would look like in a skirt, and fuck, I just realized I haven't said anything.

"Miss Graham?" I stand and make my way towards her, holding my hand out which she takes and gives me a firm handshake.

Her lips are painted bright red and I already know it's going to be an arduous task to keep from staring at her mouth. She smiles and it has my heart skipping a beat.

Christ, get it the fuck together, Wes.

"Please, take a seat," I tell her as I take my seat back behind my desk which thankfully will conceal my erection should one arise.

She sits. "Thank you so much for seeing me. I am really excited for the opportunity." She smiles again. Fuck, I wish she'd stop smiling at me like that.

I nod at her, having completely forgotten what I'm supposed to be asking her that isn't 'would you like to have dinner with me?' "Ummm," I look away from her, hoping that not staring at her will allow me to collect my thoughts. "So, tell me about yourself."

"Well, I recently graduated from Penn State. I was a business major with a double minor in Economics and French."

Fuck me, she speaks French? *"You speak French?"*

"Oui, mais pas bien." She giggles. {Yes, but not well}.

Christ.

"I understand it and can write it much better than I can speak it." She smiles and I'm still trying to calm my dick down just hearing her speak those four words, which sounded sexy as fuck.

"Well, I think that sounded great. Tell me something else about yourself? Are you from Philadelphia?" And what the fuck does that have to do with the job? *"We just need someone who understands the area."* And that's a lie.

"Oh! Yes, I'm from here. Well, technically, I was born in Seattle, because my dad played for the Seahawks but he got traded to the Eagles when I was three."

"Wait…" I blink at her. "Your father is…Theo Graham?"

"Oh, I thought you knew? Human Resources knew, I figured they'd passed that information along."

"Wow. I am a huge fan of your dad."

"I'll be sure to tell him." She smiles.

Don't look at her mouth, Wes.

"That must have been really amazing growing up in that environment."

She shrugs. "Cooler for my brother. I never really got into football. Going to games is always fun though."

"I remember the game when your dad retired."

She beams with pride. "Me too. It was a great game. Even though he destroyed his shoulder, he doesn't regret a second of it."

The words are on the tip of my tongue that I have box seats and I'd love to take her to a game before I realize, one, she probably also has box seats, and two, she's interviewing to be my fucking assistant.

I think I blacked out for the rest of the interview, but I remember offering her the job on the spot and personally showing her around the rest of the day. *Something I never do.*

And then over the past six months, I've grown to be more enthralled with her. Sometimes, I'd have no reason to walk by her desk and I'd find myself trying to come up with them. Some mornings, when I didn't have anything specific for her to do, I'd call her into my office to ask her to get me coffee just so I'd have a reason to see her and hear her voice.

"Damn, you've got it bad," Christopher says as he stares at me. I drop my head into my hands and pull my glasses from my face.

"I am going fucking insane over how much I want her. Is that possible?"

"Yes, women were put on the earth to drive us crazy. You have met my ex-wife, correct?"

I snort, thinking about the very tumultuous relationship Chris has with his ex-wife. "You cheated on her…more than once."

He points at me. "Two things can be true at once. She *was* crazy and just a nightmare. You remember."

I roll my eyes at him, not wanting to go down this road with him again. "Raegan isn't crazy. I'm the one that's crazy. I feel fucking unhinged. And I swear that Patterson kid needs to keep his eyes to himself."

"Now, he *can* actually be with her," he says taking another puff of his cigar.

"You want to live to see Christmas?" I snap, not wanting to think about him touching her or asking her out. *Maybe she's into him.* I ball my hands into a fist and try to remind myself of the fuck ton of paperwork there would be for punching that kid in the face.

He chuckles. "I'm going back inside. I need another drink. Take some deep breaths and come back in and don't beeline for Raegan when you do."

I'm outside for only a few minutes when I decide I should probably go back in, but when I turn around, I see Raegan standing at the entrance to the patio holding one of the cranberry bourbon sours. The light from the moon reflects off her silvery skirt making her shimmer.

"You were right, it's pretty good," she says as she moves onto the patio and stands next to me. Even with her heels, she only comes to my shoulders and I give myself exactly one second to think about how perfect she'd fit in my arms.

How perfect I'd fit between her legs.

"What are you doing out here?" I ask her, wondering why she's not with her friends.

"Well, Marissa is on the dance floor and I didn't really feel up to dancing." She takes a sip of her drink and I try not to pay attention to her mouth or the red lipstick that accentuates her full lips. "And I don't really feel comfortable around anyone without Marissa." I frown, wondering who has made her feel uncomfortable. She must read my face because she shakes her head. "Let me rephrase that. I just meant, I'm still so new and I just haven't gotten to know everyone yet. But everyone has been really nice."

"Good. I would hate to have to fire anyone for not playing nice in the sandbox."

She laughs, but I'm not kidding; anyone that is rude to her is gone.

"Well, that's rich," she says and I raise an eyebrow at her, willing her to go on. "Marissa said you screamed at her on her first day. That's certainly not very nice."

I cross my arms. "Did she tell you why?" *I honestly couldn't say; I have a very short fuse.*

She narrows her eyes and purses her lips into the cutest fucking scowl. "No, but that's not the point. You should apologize. It was her first day!"

I raise an eyebrow at her. "You want me to apologize?"

She shrugs and leans against the railing. "Marissa says you are grumpy towards everyone but me..." She cocks her head to the side, and I'm having a hard time gauging how much she's had to drink. If this curiosity is fueled by alcohol or maybe...*something else?* "Why is that?"

"Why do you think?" I cock my head, matching hers.

Her blue eyes narrow and she scrunches her nose and I find myself again tracing my gaze over the freckles that sit on the bridge of it. "I...I'm not sure."

I slide my hands into my pockets to stop from touching her. "Sure, you do. You graduated top of your class."

A pretty pink tinges her cheeks and I don't think I've ever seen her blush before. Now I want to know if the rest of her skin pinkens just like that. "I don't know men as well as I know business."

I nod at her drink. "How many of those have you had?"

"This is my first."

"And before that?"

She tucks a strand of her dark shiny hair behind her ear revealing a diamond stud earring. "A vodka soda and a glass of champagne."

I narrow my eyes at her because I don't know where that leaves her in terms of her judgment. "Walk a straight line."

"Excuse me?" She laughs and just the sight of her lips ticking upwards has me begging my dick to stay down.

"I want to make sure you're not intoxicated."

She sets her drink down on a nearby table and crosses her arms over her chest. "Why?"

"You can know why after you do it."

She narrows her eyes at me and begins walking a straight line perfectly before she turns around and holds her hands out. "Now tell me."

I let out a breath, wanting to be a man of my word but also not wanting to unleash all my complicated feelings on this woman I can't even touch. *Fuck it.* "I…can't stop thinking about you," I tell her honestly. "Since the moment you walked into my office." Her breath hitches and she sinks her teeth into her bottom lip as her lips quirk up in a smile. "But I can't. We can't." Her smile fades and I realize she does want me too. *You're going to have to push for it then, Raegan. I can't. There's too much at stake.* "God, I want to. But…we would both be in a lot of trouble."

"I see."

"But I wanted you to know." I shake my head at her. "You are stunning and brilliant and confident and you have this energy about you that I can't get enough of. You consume my thoughts, Raegan."

"Wes…" She starts and it's the first time she's said my name. A vision of her screaming it out while she climaxes all over my dick flashes through my brain.

I shake my head. "We should get back inside."

We begin walking back when she stops in her tracks. "What was the point in telling me all of this?"

"Because I couldn't hold it in any longer." I turn around and give her a smirk. "Besides, you already knew."

I'm trying my best to keep my eyes off of Raegan who's across the room talking to Liam Patterson *again,* and I feel almost irate at the thought of her going home with him. I'm not completely oblivious to what happens at these parties and while Liam seems like a good kid for the most part, I do know he has a bit of a reputation for sleeping with women in the office.

Don't fall for that shit, Raegan.

I wish I could tell her. I wish I could tell her to just wait until she's done working for me and finds a new job so then I can finally ask her out.

But in terms of business that would be the worst move. Raegan is smart, insightful, hardworking, and driven with a long list of other attributes that make her a model employee. I'd be stupid to let her go because I want to forge a relationship with her.

She may not even want a relationship with you! You're twenty years older than her.

Fine, because I want to fuck her?

Either way, I can't lose the best assistant I've ever had because I'm too busy thinking with my dick.

"This is the longest I think I've ever seen you at a party," I hear from next to me and when I turn my head, I find Julianne Tanner, the very young wife of the vice president of marketing who spends more time at these functions flirting and talking to everyone than with her husband. It hasn't been confirmed that she cheated on him, but it's surely been rumored.

"Mrs. Tanner." I nod, already wanting to be away from her incessant flirting. "It's lovely to see you, how are you?"

"Oh, you know." She shrugs and takes a long sip of her drink before letting her gaze move unashamedly over me. Her teeth find her lower lip and I realize she's had one too many drinks. It's definitely time for me to go.

"Well, I should—"

"Wait," she grabs my arm and I give her a look. I can't exactly reprimand her for her behavior given that she doesn't work for me, but I'll only allow this nonsense to go so far. She removes her hand. "I want to ask you something…about my husband?"

I scan the room, looking for her husband when I meet Raegan's eyes. Her eyes dart to the woman next to me and then back to me and I look down at Julianne who's looking up at me and then back at Raegan.

So, she's bothered by this.

I try to ignore the feeling that Raegan is a little jealous of my paying attention to another woman whom I'm sure she assumes is single and maybe available for me to pursue.

I'm vaguely aware that she's started talking but my eyes are still on Raegan, who's turned back to Liam though I'm grateful that it's grown into a bigger circle so maybe he's not convincing her to go home with him.

"Mrs. Tanner, if you'll excuse me," I say, without another

word or even a glance in her direction as I move towards Raegan. Chris said I shouldn't approach her, but it's a group of at least six people from my team, all of whom will be in Miami next week. *Nothing strange about that.*

"How's everyone enjoying themselves?" I ask as I approach them. Two of the women in the circle stare at me like they're starstruck, Marissa does her best to hide her grin, and Liam gives me a look that I can't quite read. *Probably because I joined the circle between him and Raegan.*

"It's always a good time. You certainly know how to throw a party," Liam says as he holds his drink up towards me. He looks around me towards Raegan, "Rae, you want to dance?"

She looks towards the dance floor and then back to him, completely avoiding my gaze.

"No," she giggles. "I don't think I'm drunk enough for that. Besides, I don't really like to dance in front of people I don't know."

"Oh, come on. Weren't you on Penn State's dance team?" He laughs and I watch as the blush finds her cheeks again but I see the brief flash of annoyance cross her face that he doesn't pick up on. *Although, I am glad that he offered up that little anecdote because I did not know that. Just when I thought she couldn't get any sexier.*

"Oh God, Liam. Leave her be, you're so annoying," Marissa groans as she crosses the circle and grabs Raegan's hand. "I have to go to the bathroom." She pulls her away and I do my best not to follow her with my gaze. The other people in the circle walk away leaving Liam and me alone, and as much as I want to walk away, I figure I should at least engage in some small talk.

"Seems like Raegan has the same effect on everyone, huh?" He says and when I meet his gaze, I'm met with knowing eyes and a smug grin.

Shit.

Chapter THREE

Raegan

I'M GRATEFUL THAT MARISSA IS DRUNKER THAN I AM, SO when we emerge from the bathroom and I happen to see Wes out of the corner of my eye in the lobby sliding on his coat, I can make up an excuse without her questioning it.

"My dad called, I'm just going to call him back," I tell her and she nods.

"I'll get you a drink!" She says before she walks back into the main room where the party is being held. Wes is already going through the revolving door so I don't bother going to get my coat even though it's fucking freezing out. I just hope that my liquor jacket will be enough for me to get him to wait. I push through the door and I'm grateful to find he's waiting for his car, but I'm really fucking annoyed that it's starting to snow and I'm wearing suede pumps.

I did not think this through.

"Wes!" I call and he spins around giving me first a surprised and then concerned look.

"Where is your coat?" He frowns, immediately pulling his off and wrapping it around me before I can protest. "It's freezing out here."

"You're leaving?" I ask. My mind momentarily goes blank as his scent wraps around me. I resist the urge to put my nose to the lapel and take a deep breath. I'm also comforted by his instinctual need to protect me and it warms me more than the coat.

"Yeah, I'm usually gone by now. People don't want to let loose with the big boss around. I like to give everyone space."

"I see." I purse my lips together. "You weren't even going to say goodbye?" I look up at him and his blue eyes are piercing and gorgeous, highlighted by his glasses.

"I'm sorry, forgive me. I'll see you on Monday." He doesn't make an effort to move and I realize it's probably in part to do with me still having his coat.

I lick my lips, hoping this doesn't come back to bite me in the ass but…he did say he wanted me. Maybe I just needed to push a little more. "Can…I come with you?"

"Raegan…"

I take a step closer to him, not close enough that we're touching but almost and I tilt my head to look up at him. "Please?"

I can see the war he's at with himself as he looks at me and then back into the venue.

"Mr. Beckham, your car, sir," I hear and I see a black Maserati pull around.

I eye it appreciatively. "Nice car."

His eyes turn to the valet attendant who's standing at his car holding his door open before moving back to mine. "I'm glad you like it."

"It's…*sexy.*"

He lets out a sigh and pinches the bridge of his nose, simultaneously pushing his glasses upward and I try to hide my smile because I think I'm about to get my way. "You're killing me, Raegan."

"My friends call me Rae."

"I definitely do *not* want to be your friend." My skin tingles in response to his words, my nipples hardening beneath my shirt. He looks behind me and then down at me again. "Where is your coat?"

"Coat check."

"Give me your ticket," he tells me.

I pull it out of my clutch and hand it to him before he ushers me into the car. He then closes the door and walks back inside.

I look around, noting how clean his car is. The inside is a rich caramel and black and it's so sleek and beautiful. Moments later, I see him moving down the stairs with my gray *Burberry* coat in his hands. He shakes hands with the guy from valet—assumedly paying him if he's anything like my dad—before he opens the back seat to lay my coat down and then slides into the driver's seat.

"Did anyone say anything to you?"

"No." He chuckles. "That's why I went in for you." He pulls out of the parking lot and I breathe a sigh of relief that we made it out with no one noticing.

"So, where are we going?" I ask.

"Where would you like to go?" he asks.

"I mean it's nearing eleven thirty, there aren't many places we could go at this hour that aren't a loud club or a bar."

"Do you want to get a drink somewhere?"

I want to tell him if the *somewhere* in question could be his house but I figure that may be too forward.

"Where were you planning to go when you left?"

"Home," he answers, and I suddenly wish I'd had another

drink because the heat crackling between us has me sobering up quick.

"Do you think it's a good idea for us to be in public together?" I counter, wanting him to come to the conclusion that it's best if we are somewhere more private.

"Everyone from the office is still at the party."

"Surely, not everyone. What if we run into someone?"

He doesn't respond right away and I'm beginning to wonder if he's not going to give into whatever urges he has. He did say *we couldn't*. Maybe he has more self-control than I thought. My eyes linger on his left hand on the steering wheel, noting the ink that peeks out from under his jacket sleeve and I'm excited to finally see how far it goes up his arm.

"I don't know that I trust myself somewhere in private with you."

"I do," I tell him. I'm not used to being forward. I had a boyfriend in high school, and two boyfriends in college, and two guys I dated casually while on the rebound from those two boyfriends, and I never made the first move. I'm not a stranger to male attention, but I am a stranger to whatever is coursing through me in response to Wes' attention. I want him and it's making me bolder than usual.

He lets out a sigh as he pulls onto the highway. It's snowing, but it's light making for an easy drive and I wonder where exactly he's taking me. "You couldn't…tell anyone."

"Not even Marissa?"

His eyes snap to mine. They're not angry but a little bit scolding. "No, not even Marissa."

I purse my lips. "Well, she thinks you've got it bad for me and I just left, and…you left, not to mention she's convinced I have a crush on you, so she *may* put two and two together."

"If you don't know how to lie convincingly, then this is not going to work." A smile tugs at his lips. "She thinks that, huh?"

"Well, clearly she was right, you did already admit you can't stop thinking about me."

He turns his gaze from the road briefly to meet mine and I see the lust written all over his face. "That's not what I meant."

I pull my hair to one side, playing with the ends nervously, not knowing what to say. "She may be correct in her theory about me."

He chuckles and takes the next exit and I still have no idea where we're going. "I see. Well, whatever does or does not happen between us outside of work, needs to stay between us, please."

I nod. "I understand."

"I'm not going to make you sign anything, but…this is serious, Raegan. I'm probably in violation of about a hundred rules just being in the car alone with you this late outside of working hours."

"I would never want to get you in trouble." I don't want to either, but if he's worried about breaking the rules and he owns the company, the consequences must be serious.

We pull into a gated community and there's a flutter in my sex thinking about the fact that he actually brought me to his house.

Oh my God.

Am I about to have sex with my boss?

"Is this okay?" He asks, the sincerity washing over me just as he pulls into his driveway, and I nod, staring at the very large house in front of me. He pulls into the garage and turns off the car before he turns to look at me. "If at any point you're uncomfortable…" he starts and I shake my head at him.

Yep. My mind thinks, in response to my earlier question.

"I'm happy you brought me here," I tell him and he smiles before getting out of the car and grabbing my coat from the back before opening my door. He helps me out and I wonder if he's nervous from the way he's acting, so I reach up and drag my hand over his jaw. He's got a very light dusting of stubble and dragging my fingertips over it sends a warm feeling shooting through me. "You're so tense. Are you nervous?"

"I've been nervous around you since the second you walked into my office." He stares down at me, his blue eyes piercing and serious and I realize I want nothing more than to feel his lips on mine.

"What?" I choke because up until this moment, he's never given me that impression. "Why?"

He takes my hand in his and pulls me towards the door in his garage leading to his house. "I tell you I can't stop thinking about you and you ask me why?"

"You're always so confident and self-assured. I didn't think..."

"What? That confident men don't get nervous around the women they can't get out of their head?"

I find myself simultaneously swooning and getting turned on by his words as he leads me into the house. Inside, I'm in shock at what I see. He's a very wealthy bachelor who owns his own company; I was picturing all white and monochromatic fixtures and stainless steel and a place that felt cold despite the warm-hearted man in front of me. What I was not expecting was an instant feeling of warmth and safety the second I walked inside. The first thing I notice is his kitchen, with hardwood floors and an island that matches with forest green accents for all of the cabinets. It's straight out of what I would picture in a cozy cottage and not this huge house. He slides his coat off of me and disappears with mine as well.

I move through the kitchen and take in his living room that has an entire wall lined with windows looking out into miles of forest. I realize now that we're on a hill, allowing me to see for miles behind his house and giving the most gorgeous view. It's begun to snow and there are flecks of white floating through the air against the black sky and greenery.

Realizing that I'm probably not going home tonight, I decide now is the time to let my dad know I'm staying at a friend's house. I pull my phone from my clutch and am just hitting send when Wes returns and his eyes drop to the phone in my hand. I wonder if he thinks I'm telling some salacious story about why exactly I left the holiday party early. "Oh, I…I'm just letting my dad know I'm not coming home. He worries." He nods and I take a step towards him. "Do you trust me?"

"I do." He nods. "I just can't believe you're actually here." He sits on his couch and part of me wants to climb into his lap. I can feel the tension radiating from him and I realize if I want him, I'm going to have to make the first move. I go to where he's seated on the couch and kneel in front of him on the floor, placing my hands on his knees and separating his legs before I move my hands up his thighs. I'm fully aware that we haven't even kissed yet, and I'm alluding that I want to put my mouth on his dick, but here we are.

"You're so tense. What can I do to help?" I reach his upper thighs and squeeze, bracketing the space around his dick and his nostrils flare as lust flashes across his handsome face.

"Raegan." He groans and when I look up at him, his icy blue eyes are full of hunger.

"Yes, Mr. Beckham?"

"You're out of your mind if you think I'm going to come before you do."

I drag my hand across his groin, grazing his dick gently with the backs of my fingers and he narrows his eyes at me. "Get up here," he grunts and I stand, reaching behind me to slide down my skirt exposing the fact that I'm wearing sheer thigh-high stockings and a pair of silk black panties edged with lace beneath my skirt.

"My skirt is too tight to straddle you," I tell him when his eyes widen and his hand reaches out to help me into his lap.

"You are exquisite, Raegan," he tells me as his hands slide up my frame. I sink down so that I'm seated directly on top of his dick, my pussy pressed against him, and on instinct, I rub against him letting out a whimper as his hardness moves along my clit even through his slacks. "Fuck." He lets out a shaky breath and the word slithers down my spine to the space between my legs like it was directed towards it. "I've never—" He lets his eyes close and his head falls back as I rub against him again. "I've owned my company for ten years and I've never wanted anyone that worked for me. Never touched anyone I shouldn't." His hands start at my knees which are bent at his hips and move up my thighs. I'm still wearing my shirt, but it stops just above my navel because my skirt was high-waisted and he traces the skin there with his index finger causing me to shiver.

"What's so special about me?" I gasp as he moves lower to drag his finger along the top of my panties—so gently, I shiver in his arms.

"Everything." His voice is low and throaty and sexy as hell.

His words send not only a spark to my sex but to my heart and even though I tell myself that this may never go further than tonight, somewhere my mind is subconsciously thinking about a future that has me and Wes and a happily ever after.

"The way you drag the tip of your pen along your bottom lip during meetings, or really anything with your mouth. You know, I can barely be in a room with you while you're eating?" He moves closer to me, his lips on my neck as he places featherlight kisses down my throat. "You always check with me before you leave when you're done for the day and if I'm still in a meeting, you'll wait. Sometimes, it's the only time I've really talked to you that day and it's usually the highlight." His tongue darts out and licks the skin he just kissed and I shiver. "You're kind without being a pushover, and as much as I hate that you work for me because it makes what we're doing right now really fucking wrong and difficult, I'm glad that you walked into my office because you're the best assistant I've ever had."

"Wes." I sigh not knowing what else to say in response to his sweet words.

"Also, you're fucking gorgeous and you make my dick harder than anyone has in years. I'm forty-one and suddenly I don't know how to control my erections." It's a swift change from his earlier words causing a fire between my legs that I'm desperate for him to put out.

Right on time, his dick jerks beneath me and I gasp at the feeling of him hardening beneath my pussy.

"Once we cross this line," he continues, "I don't know what's going to happen." His hand moves up my body and finds my cheek, cupping it gently. "Tell me what you want."

I lean forward and brush my lips gently across his. "The same things you want." I move in his lap again and goosebumps pop up everywhere in response to the light kiss coupled with the less than light dry humping.

"Which is? I need you to say it," he presses.

Okay, I guess I need to be clearer than taking my skirt off. "I'm sitting on top of you, wet and throbbing and you think I don't want you to fuck me?"

He bites down on his lower lip before dragging a finger across it and *fuck if he doesn't look sexy.* He looks down between us at where I'm sitting on top of him before his gaze meets mine. "I don't want you to feel like I…coerced you."

"Wes," I grab his jaw, making him look at me. "I don't feel coerced and I would never screw you over. I want this." A look of relief crosses his face, and I rub my nose against his lightly letting out a soft giggle that makes his cock twitch beneath me. "You're so freaking cute."

He chuckles just as his hands find my ass and grip it hard. "Cute?"

"Well, you're gorgeous and sexy and you have a way of making my panties damp with just a look, but yes you're also cute because you're taking the time to make sure I'm okay with all of this and that I don't feel taken advantage of." I reach for his tie, slowly undoing the knot and sliding it off of him. "Again, I don't." He nods as I unbutton the top button of his dress shirt and then the second and then the third. "I asked to come home with you." I press my lips to the skin I've just exposed before letting my tongue dart out to lick the skin. "I took my skirt off and climbed into your lap." I move back onto his thighs so I can unbuckle his belt and pants before pulling his shirt out. I unbutton the rest of the buttons putting his bare chest on display and I drag my eyes slowly down his body.

I lick my lips and his hand reaches for my chin, lifting it so my eyes meet his. "There's one more thing we should talk about first."

"Okay?" I don't think I've ever had a guy preface so many things before hooking up with him but then again, I've never hooked up with my billionaire boss either. Not that money really impresses me, having grown up with no shortage of it, but I can definitely tell the difference in his level of wealth. Not to mention, he doesn't have two children that I know put a significant dent in my father's net worth.

"I have a piercing."

My mouth drops open and my eyes widen to the size of saucers. "You have a what?!" I squeal as I scramble off his lap and to my knees in front of him to continue pulling off his pants. This man, this grumpy, straight-laced man that is somehow soft for *me*, has his dick pierced? *Oh, my fucking God.* "Let me see it."

His hand reaches for my hair, running his fingers through

it gently and I fucking melt because I love when a guy plays with my hair. "I just wanted to prepare you."

I shove his hands out of the way as if they're trying to slow me down. "Consider me prepared; let me *see* it." My eyes dart up to his. "I've never seen one before." I let out a breath, suddenly a little nervous. "I know it can feel good...for you and for me." I bite my bottom lip. "I just don't want an instance like from the movie *The Sweetest Thing*." I shudder thinking about how the hell I'd explain to my dad that I had to go to the hospital because my boss's dick piercing was lodged behind my tonsils.

"Relax, honey, that's only happened once."

"What?!" I squeal, staring at him in horror.

He chuckles instantly and I realize he's kidding by the playful glint in his eye. "That was a joke. It's never happened. With my piercing, it would be hard for it to get caught on anything."

"All this talk about it is making me wet." I press my hand to his groin and unzip his pants before reaching inside, my hand immediately wrapping around his dick as best as I can while he still has his briefs on. I drag my thumb along it, fumbling for something that feels metal and out of the ordinary when I feel two metal balls one at the tip and one on the upper side of his shaft.

Fuck. Me.

My mouth drops open and I look up at him. "Take off your pants. *Now.*"

Chapter FOUR

WES

I'M STARING DOWN AT RAEGAN WHO'S KNEELING BETWEEN my legs, her hand still inside of my pants dragging her thumb over my piercings with the most curiously sexy expression. I stand up, effectively removing her hand from my pants, zipping them back up, and pulling her to her feet. "No."

"No?"

"No," I repeat. "I need to get well acquainted with your pussy first and I won't be able to once you see it and want to spend the rest of the night figuring out how it works."

"How it…works?" She raises an eyebrow.

"Yes. How it feels in your hands, your mouth, your pussy. How good it feels to rub the metal ball against your clit. Trust me, there's a lot you're going to want to try." I pull her hard against me, reaching around to pluck the string nestled between her ass cheeks, "and I want to taste your pussy first."

She gasps just as I lift her into my arms and her legs immediately wrap around my back as I walk through the living room and up my staircase. Her lips go to my neck and the space behind my ear where she lets out a moan every few seconds that's making me harder with each step.

"Wes," she moans in my ear. It's breathy and sexy and reminds me that I haven't really kissed her yet, and I don't want to take another step without doing so. We are halfway up my stairs on the first landing when I push her against the wall and seal my mouth over hers. I'm very aware that her pussy covered by only a thin layer of lace, is pressed directly against my bare torso and as she rubs against me, I feel her wet heat against me.

I feed her my tongue, stroking hers gently at first and then harder as hers tangles with mine and it's better than any fantasy I've ever had of her and I like this. I've pictured kissing her hundreds of times. Every time she moans and whimpers under my tongue but nothing could prepare me for the rubbing of her wet cunt against my torso while she does it. "Wes, take me to your bedroom, *please*," she begs. "I need you."

I've had this vision too; her begging for my dick and for me to fuck her across my desk just moments after I've had my mouth on her cunt.

I pull away from that sinful mouth and press my lips to the skin just above where her pulse flickers in her neck. "You do, huh?" I keep moving up the stairs and she manages to push my shirt off of me, letting it fall to the floor as I continue ascending the stairs. Her eyes immediately go to the sleeve of ink on my arm and her teeth sink into her bottom lip just as I carry her into my bedroom. I'm used to some sort of reaction to my tattoos, but Raegan's eyes light up with a mix of lust and curiosity and it makes me even harder that she's intrigued. I turn on the lights, choosing the dimmest setting to allow just enough light for us to ogle each other as I set her on the edge of my bed.

Her eyes are still on me and I'm staring at her shirt like it's offensive. "Take off your shirt."

"Take off your pants," she responds immediately and when I don't make a move, she huffs at me before pulling her shirt over her head. I don't even have to tell her about her bra which is sexy as fuck for the record—black and lace and see through—before she unclasps it and hands it to me in the same polite way she hands me my coffee in the mornings.

I drop to my knees, wanting to be eye level—*well mouth level really*—with Raegan's breasts and more importantly her rosy pink nipples that are begging to be sucked. "You have the prettiest tits," I tell her without pulling my eyes from them.

"Thank you," she whispers and then a moan leaves her lips the second I put my hand on her breast and strum my thumb over her nipple. I grab the other, palming them both and stroking her nipples as they turn to stiff peaks in my hands. Her head is thrown back, her legs spread allowing me to settle between them, and I don't miss the subtle moving of her hips upwards towards me as I fondle her tits. I wrap an arm around her back and then I press my lips to her chest, licking a path up between the valley of her breasts.

"Wes," she cries out when my lips find her nipple, my tongue circling it before I bite down gently. She gasps, "oh my God!" She looks down at me, just as I look up and note the flush in her cheeks. "Do that again," she whispers.

"You like when I bite these pretty little nipples?" My dick throbs thinking about leaving teeth marks on them. Hickeys she'll see in the morning reminding her of tonight and whose mouth was on them.

She nods. "I—I didn't know I liked that."

I move to her other breast, giving it the same attention,

licking and nipping at the skin before sucking her nipple into my mouth and biting down. "No one has ever played with your tits like this?" My hand is on the other one and I roll the nipple between my thumb and index finger in time with what I'm doing to the one in my mouth.

"N—no," she stammers. "Wes, *please* I want more."

I groan against her skin. "You smell so good." I drag my mouth away from her tits and down her stomach to the space just above her mound. "I can smell how much you want me."

"*Yes.*" I take my time sliding her thigh-highs off and letting them drop to the floor. "Wes, oh my God, please fuck me."

"Oh, we are a long way from that, Raegan." I chuckle, wondering how in the hell she got the idea that I'd be sticking my dick inside of her pussy before my tongue got a taste.

"But..."

"You want to see my dick?" I stand up in front of her and watch as her eyes dart to my groin. She reaches out for me and I take a step back out of her reach. "I want something first."

"Okay, whatever it is, done."

"I hope this isn't how you negotiate." I chuckle and she glares at me.

"Stop being a tease! You said you wanted me and you're toying with me." She stands up, reaching for me again, and again I back up.

"You didn't even hear my terms." I tut at her and look at her from over my glasses, then I watch as she sits back down and presses her legs together. "Before you can see my dick, Raegan Graham, you need to come. In my mouth. *Twice.*" I unzip my slacks and force them down leaving me in gray briefs that I'm actually rather grateful I'd chosen to wear versus black ones. The material does nothing to hide my size or the hardness or the wetness from my cock leaking from the tip in response to everything that's happened between us tonight. There's a wet spot and I watch her lick her lips lasciviously before raising an eyebrow like she thinks she could break me before adhering to my terms.

"You're hard."

I pull off my glasses and toss them on the bed. "The most beautiful woman I've ever met is practically naked and sitting on my bed, of course, I'm hard."

"I could help with that."

"I'm sure you could," I tell her as I get back on my knees in front of her. "But nothing matters at this moment except tasting your cunt, and *yes,* that includes learning what your mouth would feel like wrapped around my cock." I expect her to protest so I swipe my tongue over her once, tasting her wetness through the silk covering her pussy, applying just enough pressure to stimulate her clit and she gasps. A smug grin finds my face at how easy it was to get my way. "God, you're so wet and I've barely touched you."

I grab her underwear at her hips, pull them down her legs, and drop them to the floor leaving the woman I haven't been able to stop thinking about for six months completely naked. Her pussy is free of any hair and while I don't have a preference, there is something about Raegan's smooth, bare cunt that makes me feel even more feral to put my mouth on her.

"You're so perfect, Raegan." I move closer to her and nibble her inner thigh at the place closest to her pussy. "I've fucked my hand so many times picturing this moment." I pull both of her legs to rest over my shoulders and blow gently on her wet slit causing her to whimper.

"Really?" She sighs.

"Fuck yes. I've pictured spreading you out on my desk while I'm on a conference call and devouring your pussy."

"You…you can still do that." When I look up at her, she's panting like she's just run a marathon.

"You'd let me fuck you with the entire office just outside my door? You know you'd have to be quiet and from what I've observed so far, you're not exactly good at that."

"Gag me, then," she sasses and my cock jerks between my legs.

"Fuck." I grit out and my eyes shut at the thought of shoving her wet panties in her mouth while I ran my tongue all over her clit. I reach for my dick, pulling it once just to try and temper the ache building in it and her eyes flit to the movement.

She runs her hand through my hair, pulling on it gently. "To answer your question, I'd let you fuck me anywhere." Her blue eyes are so vulnerable but sexy and I try not to let myself get lost in them. "I never see you without your glasses. You have really beautiful eyes."

I grab her hand from my head and brush my lips over her knuckles. "I was just thinking the same about yours."

I hear the faintest warning from within that I'm already in too deep with Raegan. That I've been consumed with her for months and now I'm preparing to lick and fuck her and that is going to do nothing for the constant thoughts of her that run through my mind on a loop every day.

I push those thoughts way the fuck out of my head because her scent is overwhelming me and if I don't slide my tongue through her slit, I'm going to lose it. My mouth waters for a taste of her as I spread her open with my fingers. I watch as goosebumps erupt on her flesh as I let my tongue ghost over her clit, teasing her, but Raegan is *not* fucking having it. She pushes her pelvis harder against my mouth and I grin against her, wanting to unleash the side of myself that wants to devour her.

"Oh my God," she cries out as I rub my tongue harder against her, exploring her, tasting her everywhere. I drag my tongue up and back from her clit down to her entrance before sliding it inside of her and she falls to her back and presses the heels of her feet into my back. "Holy shit." I continue fucking her with my tongue as I drag my thumb up to rub her clit in circles that has her raising her hips to meet my face. "God, that feels good."

I move my tongue back to her clit and her hands move back to my hair, tightening her grip on the strands. The feeling goes right to my dick like her hand is wrapped around it too. "Wes, oh my God, I'm going to come."

My knee-jerk reaction is to tell her *I know.* That I feel her shaking and her grip tightening on my hair as she keeps my mouth where she wants it, but I just hum against her, sending a vibration through her that has her screaming.

"Oh God, right there, holy fuck, Wes, your mouth," she says followed by a pornstar-worthy moan. Her voice is low and breathy and at this point my dick is tingling to the point of almost pain with how desperate I am to be inside of her. Her taste, her sounds, everything about her is turning me on. It only takes one more swipe of my tongue for her to go over the edge moaning my name through her climax. Her legs stiffen and her heels press harder against me.

She sits up, leaning on her elbows as she gives me a smirk. Her eyes are shining and her dark hair is slightly disheveled. "Wow. That was intense." I don't move from my place, hovering a mere inch above her sex even as she tries to reach for me.

I shake my head at her. "Give me another one."

"Wes…"

"I said two." I eye her hungrily. "I need another one."

"You *need* it?" She narrows her eyes into slits as she grips my chin and runs her thumb over my wet bottom lip. "More than you need to come down my throat?"

I didn't think my dick could get harder, but it does in response to her filthy words. "Don't argue with me, you agreed to the terms."

"No, I didn't."

I ignore her as I press my lips back to pussy, eating her more aggressively than I had before. I knew I already wanted more. It only took one time for me to be addicted to her sexy sweet taste and now I'm already thinking of all the different places where I can secretly get my mouth between her legs. I want her on my desk, hers too, and the table in the conference room. I want to stop the elevator while a group of people wait just a floor below because I can't even wait to get to my office to get my hands on her. I want to defile every inch of *Beckham Securities* with her despite the one hundred rules in place that forbid just that. I want to defile every inch of *her* all over *Beckham Securities.*

The thought that she's flying to Miami early with me on Wednesday floats through my head and I already can't wait to fuck her in the bedroom of my private jet.

I reach a hand up to palm her breast and pinch one of her nipples and a squeal leaves those pouty lips letting me know that she's close and part of me wonders if she'll let me do this a third time. "Fuck, you already know my body so well."

"Your body responds so well to me," I say as I continue to lap at her pussy.

"It has for months."

My ears perk up at that because *excuse me?* I make a mental note to go back to that because I can tell she's nearing her second climax. I reach under her ass to cup each cheek as I push my face harder into her sex and continue to rub my tongue all over her. She's so fucking sweet and I already know I'm going to be pawing at her daily for another taste of her.

Fuck. Fuck. Fuck.

It wasn't enough that I crossed this line with someone I had no business crossing it with. But now I know what her cunt tastes like and I won't be able to get it out of my head.

Much like her.

"Honey, I need you to come. I need to taste your orgasm." And I can hear the begging in my voice.

"God, yes. I want to come in your mouth…" Her eyes drop to meet mine. "And on your face."

"Fuck." I grunt, thinking about her pussy resting on top of my mouth. "Yes." I growl as my mind goes blank and I can't focus on anything except Raegan and her pussy and the sexy sounds she's making right now. "I want you to sit on my face and rub this sticky, sweet cunt all over my mouth."

"Oh God…keep…talking…" she chokes out.

So, she likes dirty talk. Like I wasn't already fucking obsessed. "You going to suck my dick while you're on top of me?"

"Yes, fucking please." She moans. "Let me taste you."

"The second you come."

She lets out another sigh and I push two fingers inside of her, curling my fingers upwards and she gasps. "Wes! Oh my God!" She cries out as a spasm wracks her tiny frame. Her hands leave my hair and go to her tits and then into her own hair. "Oh fuck, I'm coming!"

And fuck, does she. I haven't been with a woman that squirted in years but she does, *hard.* I pull back slightly at some point to really see it up close and some drips down my chin to my chest. My eyes light up because watching her orgasm leak out of her might be the hottest thing I've ever witnessed.

I kiss her through her orgasm, and when she pushes my face away from her sex with a moan that toys with the rest of my resolve, I stand up. "Holy fuck, Raegan." I lick my lips and wipe my mouth with my hand, doing my best to collect most of the juices. "You squirt."

Her eyes are still closed. She's still trying to catch her breath, but her eyes flutter open and she sits up slowly. "I do? I did?" She looks down between her legs at the wet spot beneath her and all over me and pink tints her cheeks. "Oh my God, I'm sorry. I... didn't know."

She didn't know about her nipples or that she squirts? Jesus, what assholes has she been sleeping with? I ignore the tinge of jealousy that shoots through me at the thought of anyone touching her.

"Honey, I loved that." I grip her chin. "It was incredibly sexy. You've never done that before?"

"No." She shakes her head.

"Well, it makes me proud as fuck that I'm the only man that's been able to make you do that."

"I'm sorry about your comforter..."

I narrow my gaze at her. "Please don't apologize. Now, I'll lay in this bed and remember your pretty pussy coming all over it." *And that's just on the nights you're not here to do it again.*

She gives me a shy smile before her eyes drop to my dick. I've made myself ignore the dull ache in my cock, but the way she's looking at it has made me painfully aware that I haven't come. She's off the bed and on her knees in front of me within a second with her hands on my waistband yanking my briefs down. My cock springs free and she gasps in shock when it juts out straight at her, grazing her lips with how close she is.

"Shit," she whispers, assumedly more to herself. She looks up at me and then back down at it. "I knew you'd have the most perfect dick." She wastes no time sliding her hand over me and dragging a finger over the silver ball at the tip and the one on the top of my shaft. "Did it hurt?"

"I was a little drunk so, no, but it's also been years." I ball my hands into fists, trying my best not to let myself think too much about the fact that the woman of my dreams has my dick in her hands.

"What made you get it?" She asks and I was not expecting this conversation right now but somehow her curiosity is making me harder than granite.

"The truth?" I ask her.

She nods. "Please."

"The girl I was seeing in college."

"Hmmm." She doesn't respond for a moment. "I'm not the jealous type," she says, "but the thought of another woman touching you..." She looks up at me and fire flashes in her eyes. "I don't like it."

"I'm ready to lose my shit the second any man at the office breathes in your direction, but it's been years, honey. Almost two decades." She nods and leans forward and I know what she wants to do and my dick is aching for it. "Do it, baby. Suck me into that warm, wet mouth and put me out of my misery, *please*."

Her tongue darts out and first traces each of the metal balls and *my* balls tingle in response. Next, she circles the tip, dragging it along her tongue and then down my shaft slowly.

"Fuck, I should have known you'd be a little tease."

"You said I could play with it," she says as she stands up. "Lay on the bed."

I narrow my gaze at her, knowing I'm in for a long night, before listening to her and she kneels between my legs instantly. "You haven't come yet, so I won't use your dick to masturbate... this time."

I groan, the words making me feel like I could explode at the thought of her dragging my piercing over her clit until she comes. "How kind of you," I grit out.

She lowers her mouth to my dick and then she wraps her

lips around the tip and pushes herself down as far as she can go. She's almost at the bottom when I feel her open up her throat and go farther. "Oh fuck, Raegan. Don't force it, baby." She ignores me, moving up and down as she sucks *hard.* I try *really* fucking hard not to move my hips but her mouth feels so fucking good and with her hand fondling my balls, in the heat of the moment, I thrust upwards.

"Fuck, baby, I'm sorry," I sputter, hoping I didn't hurt her. I'm not exactly small and I know she's not used to having something metal tap the back of her throat. *Jesus, Wes. Don't choke her.*

She pulls me out of her mouth, a sexy trail of spit connecting her mouth to my dick. "Sorry for what?" She cocks her head to the side and wipes the tears forming under her eyes. "I want you to lose control. I want you to fuck my face," she purrs. "Use my mouth to make you come."

"Not in your mouth," I grunt.

She frowns. "Why not?"

"I want to come while I'm fucking your pussy. I want the first time I come to be in response to your pussy coming all over my dick." She gasps but then it's like she remembers something because she furrows her brow and starts to nibble on her bottom lip. "What is it, honey?"

"I don't...I mean I haven't...I don't usually...during sex." She finally gets out and her cheeks turn the brightest shade of pink as she looks everywhere but me.

I touch her face, tilting it towards me. "Ever?"

She shakes her head. "I can other ways just not...from penetration."

"Well, it's been obvious to me you've been sleeping with the wrong guys. Can I try anyway?"

She suddenly looks shy and a little nervous but she nods. "Sorry, did I totally kill the mood?"

I look down at my dick and then back at her. "You see how hard I still am, right? Trust me Raegan, if you're naked and in my sight, I'm in the mood." I run my hand over her pert nipple. "If you're wearing a parka, and in my sight, I'm in the mood."

She blinks those gorgeous eyes at me and gives me a sexy smile before going back to my dick. She continues working me up and down which I let go on for longer than I expect. "Okay, that's enough," I grunt out. My dick screams at me and I realize it's going to be even angrier as I remember I have to go to the bathroom for a condom. I get off the bed and she gasps.

"Where are you going?"

"I need to get a condom."

"Oh." She lets out a breath and nods in agreement. I'm back after grabbing the box from my bathroom in case we need more in a few hours or in the morning and pull one out. I'm opening it when I see her staring at my dick in fascination and maybe a little…disappointment?

"Talk to me, what is it, honey? Are you nervous?"

"No…I just…I kind of wanted to see what it felt like…" She looks up at me. "Without one…just for a second?"

I swallow and my cock officially feels like it could explode at the thought of fucking her raw. I let out a shaky breath. "Are you on birth control?"

She winces and shakes her head. "No."

I let out another breath because I'm too far into the haze of overwhelming lust that is telling me to not only fuck her raw but come inside of her in hopes she'll get pregnant.

Where the hell did that come from?

"Right, stupid," she says, clearly taking my silence as something completely different.

"I need to be on top," I tell her as I toss the condom somewhere, *no idea where.* I worry that if she's on top, she may be too caught up in the moment and not heed my warning in time that I'm about to come.

"Wh—what?"

"I'm not going to come inside of you."

"But I'm not—"

"Which is why I'm not going to come inside of you, but you said you wanted to feel all of me." She blinks at me like she hasn't put together that I'd do anything she asked me to do.

I'm on top of her instantly, my dick resting against her stomach. "You sure this is what you want?"

"Yes." She bites her bottom lip. "I haven't…I mean, I've been tested since my last relationship."

"I wasn't worried." I drop my lips to her neck as I swipe my dick through her slit and let out a groan. "You shouldn't be either by the way."

"I don't think you'd ever do anything to hurt me," she whispers and I nod, our eyes already having the unspoken conversation that I'm not ready to have out loud.

"Raegan, if I don't get inside your cunt right fucking now, I'm going to lose my mind." I pull back to look at her. "Are you ready?"

She nods. "Yes, I want you so badly, Wes. I want you to fuck me hard. *Please,*" she begs me.

I press a kiss to the space between her breasts again before I drag my tongue up the skin and into her mouth just as I push my way inside of her.

Immediately, my eyes slam shut and fireworks go off behind my eyelids because *holy fucking hell.* I'm acutely aware that she's moaning my name as she claws at my back. "Jesus, Raegan, you're so fucking tight," I whisper as I drag my tongue gently across the seam of her lips. I don't move as I try to let her—*and mostly myself*—adjust. "You, okay?"

"Yes, I'm so fucking okay, but I need you to move, Wes, *please.*"

"I need a second or I'm going to fucking explode and I would like to thrust more than once before I need to pull out." *Fuck, I almost wish I had a condom on because the thought of having to pull out of Raegan's tight, warm cunt sounds like my worst nightmare.*

"I've never felt this before," she whispers. "I feel so full and you're so...*deep.*"

Ah, so maybe it was their dicks that were the problem.

"I can feel every ridge of you and your piercing." I pull back and slowly push back in. "Oh my God, that feels good. Do that again."

I start to push in and out of her now that I've gotten a hold on my emotions and more importantly my dick.

Her arms are wrapped around my neck and her lips are pressed to the space behind my ear, licking and sucking the skin there as she meets my thrusts. She jerks her hips up to meet me, her cunt squeezing me every time I bottom out inside of her. She lets out a moan and her lips move from my neck and collide with mine, sliding her tongue against mine as she whimpers every few thrusts.

Christ, she feels good.

I feel that familiar feeling creeping up my spine and the blaring warning that I need to pull out when she locks her ankles behind my back. She pulls away from my lips, and I'm transfixed by how swollen and shiny and red they are. Her blue eyes are wide and are glazed over like she's holding back tears. "Wes, I think I'm going to come," she whispers just as her eyes flutter shut. "Oh God, yes. Right there." She clamps down on me and her fingernails dig into my shoulders as her climax washes over her. "Wes! Oh my God, yes yes yes." She cries out and it's taking every ounce of willpower I have not to unleash my orgasm inside of her.

I drop my hand to her clit to coax out the aftershocks as I pull out of her and shoot my cum all over her stomach. "Fuck, Raegan." I grit out as I use one hand to pump myself and the other to rub her sweet clit.

She looks down at the mess I've made on her and then up into my eyes and I briefly wonder if she's upset when a smile finds her face. "That is so hot." She drags her middle finger through it and sucks it into her mouth all while her eyes never leave mine. "I knew you'd taste good. Next time, I'd like to try it from the source."

My cock twitches and when her eyes shoot to the movement, she raises an eyebrow at me.

I let out a breath before I lean down to press a kiss to her lips. "Let me clean you up first." I grab a washcloth and run it under warm water and when I move back into the room, she's staring at me with the sweetest expression. I kneel next to her and begin cleaning her off.

"Wes, that was incredible." She bites down on her bottom lip. "I've never…" She sits up once I'm finished and climbs into my lap.

"Ah, that's right, you said you don't normally come during sex, but it seems you can. I'm beginning to think you were just trying to challenge me," I joke, but she shakes her head, her eyes serious and fixed on me.

"It's never been like that for me."

"It's never been like that for me either." I rub my lips over hers, hoping that makes it very clear that I want more of this and her.

She sighs against my lips. "How long until we can do it again?"

Chapter FIVE

Raegan

I WAKE UP THE NEXT MORNING, MY ENTIRE BODY deliciously sore with the man responsible wrapped tightly around me. I'm on my side and he's pressed into my back with a hand around my middle and I can hear him snoring lightly behind me. I desperately need to use the bathroom so I untangle myself as best I can from him, grateful he doesn't wake up before I move into his bathroom. My hair is still wet from the shower we took together last night but he brushed it out for me after, so thankfully, it's not a total rat's nest.

I grab the toothbrush he'd given me and wash my face, ecstatic that he actually has face wash and not just a bar of soap. After I'm finished in the bathroom, I see he's still sleeping, which I'm not surprised about; I'm fairly certain the sun was starting to rise when we finally finished fooling around. I'm still naked and without his body heat, a little bit cold. My eyes snap to the view outside his window and I blanche looking at the snow pouring from the gray sky. I can already hear my dad now.

Stay there or I'm coming to get you. Do not Uber or let one of your friends drive.

I wince as I grab my phone, and surely enough I have a text from my dad this morning saying just that.

Sure, Dad. Please come get me from my boss' house who I spent the night with having the best sex of my life. Did I mention it's totally against the rules, I could probably get fired, and I'm really into him?

I move to the other end of his bedroom to his closet and am truly in awe at the size of it. I run my fingers over his rows of suits and dress shirts noting that everything is organized by color and then by style. I spy some sweatpants that I know will be huge but I pull them on, tying them as tightly as possible to keep them on and a Harvard business school sweatshirt.

I make my way out of the closet and note that he's still asleep, still curled around the space where I was, and is now using the pillow I slept on. I grab my phone before quietly slipping out of the room and down the stairs because one, I'm starving, and two, Wes gets a little hangry in the mornings. I open the refrigerator spotting some eggs and bacon and more importantly, the coffee maker on the counter. I consider making him pancakes for about half a second because that's a risky choice based on how inconsistent I am with them. Half the time they're perfect, and half the time it takes me fourteen tries just to get two that are edible.

I can almost hear Avery's mom, who runs the best café in town in my ear telling me not to over stir the batter and that it's *not* time to flip it—*while I'm in the middle of flipping it.*

Eggs are easy and I know how he likes them. I start on the bacon first so the eggs don't get cold and it only takes about five minutes after the smell of it wafts through the kitchen to feel hands wrapped around me and lips at my neck. I giggle thinking about what my grandma always said: "*There's two ways to wake a man up in the morning, sex and the smell of bacon.*"

"You're in my clothes and cooking me breakfast. Are you trying to seduce me? If you wanted sex, you should have woken me up." He presses a kiss to my cheek and I turn to face him.

"I was freezing and hungry." I touch my nose and it still feels a little cold despite standing at the stove. "What do you keep the temperature at?"

He chuckles and moves around the corner. "Thermostat is over here." When he comes back around the corner, I shoot him a glare. "I turned it up!"

"What was it at?" I narrow my gaze at him.

"Sixty-five."

"During a blizzard?!" I say gesturing towards his window.

"I get really hot." He shrugs as he starts brewing himself some coffee.

"Yes, because that's *so* indicative of the way you were sleeping literally on top of me!" I say, sarcastically. "That is too cold. I am never coming over again."

He rolls his eyes. "Sure, honey." The thought that it's already a foregone conclusion in his mind that I'd be back sends a sizzle through me and I turn back to the bacon. "You know, when you're here, you're not my assistant. You aren't responsible for making me breakfast."

"I know, but I'm not making breakfast for my boss. I'm making it for the guy that gave me multiple orgasms last night."

He presses a kiss to the side of my head. "Well, he appreciates it."

I start making his eggs, as I pull the last of the bacon out of the pan and put some bread in his toaster. "So, not to totally overstay my welcome but my dad will have a fit if I come home right now with the way the roads are and I'm not about to ask him to come get me. So, would you mind if I hung out for a bit?" I say without turning around. I know he's attracted to me, but I also know he's busy and may not want someone hanging out in his space all day regardless of the amazing sex.

"You could never overstay your welcome and you are absolutely not leaving right now." When I turn around, he's looking at me from over his glasses. "I can take you home later or tomorrow. They say it should stop tonight."

Tomorrow?!

I turn back to the stove. "Okay," I smile with glee and breathe a quiet sigh of relief when I realize I cooked his over-easy egg perfectly and didn't break the yolk. I put everything on a plate and slide it in front of him before I begin scrambling my eggs. A few minutes later, I'm seated next to him and it just feels so *domestic.* Sitting here with him. In his house. On a Saturday morning.

"So, what do you normally do on weekends?" I say as I pull the mug to my lips.

He takes a sip of his coffee. "Work mostly. During the summer and early fall I play golf. In the winter sometimes I'll go watch college football at a bar or with Chris. I went to the University of Michigan and since you went to Penn State, I'm sure I don't have to tell you that football is kind of a religion."

"You do remember who my dad is right? Football was kind of a religion before I could walk."

He laughs. "Of course."

"I can remember more than one Christmas I spent in a box suite actually." A faint smile finds my lips because although it's not a particularly painful memory, it just serves as a reminder of how different my life was compared to my friends.

"What was that like?"

"It was okay." I shrug. I really only open this box when I'm talking to my therapist and I haven't talked to her in months.

Hmm, reminder to circle back to that.

"I definitely preferred the holidays we spent with my uncle and aunt and my grandparents when everyone lived here. If my dad was playing on Thanksgiving or Christmas Day, it was usually just me and Lucas and him."

"Are you close with your brother?" He asks and I nod, remembering the years we weren't but how things changed the second I got my license and he needed a ride. *Then I was suddenly the best sister in the world.*

"Yeah, he's like my best friend now. Pain in my ass though." I chuckle. "He's about a year and a half younger than me, so you can imagine in our later teen years we had practically all the same friends and went to the same parties. He's a junior at NYU now and he's killing it. I'm so proud of him. He comes home this week and I'm really excited. It's weird being home and he's not here." I turn to look at him and note that he's staring at me intently. "Sorry, I'm rambling." I giggle nervously and he shakes his head.

"I could listen to you talk all day." He smiles and I have to actively stop myself from squealing because, *God, he's sweet.* "And it's refreshing, being able to listen and not having to talk so much."

"What about you?" I ask. "Do you have siblings?"

"No, just me, but I always wanted a brother," he says. "Or a sister, really. Just someone to talk to while I was at home. I think that's why I did so well in school. I was so bored at home, all I did was study."

"Were your parents not around?"

"They were and they were great but, you know it's not the same."

"I get it. Did you have a lot of friends? I imagine you being so popular." I laugh thinking about him being captain of a sports team and the guy all of the girls wanted to date.

"I did have friends but I wouldn't call myself popular. Like I said, I was always studying. So, there were many parties and things I missed out on because I was so focused on school."

"Your parents must have been so proud of you."

"Yeah, eventually." He nods and I wonder if there is more to that story. "My parents were young when they had me and I think they were just caught up in their own lives for a while. They weren't bad parents, just…a little checked out sometimes. They always showed up but it was usually between their things and I sometimes felt like I was just something to check off their list to prove they had done good parenting that day." He leans forward, his eyes not on me, and narrows them slightly. "I don't usually talk about them this early on with someone."

"Oh. I'm sorry. I didn't mean to pry." I wince because I'm the same way when it comes to talking about my mother. It usually takes a few shots of tequila for me to be really comfortable with someone to unleash the Rebecca Graham saga.

His eyes snap to mine and his hand reaches up to rub my cheek, then his lips press against mine gently. "No," he says when he pulls away. "I feel comfortable with you."

"Me too." I drop my hand to his thigh and rub it gently before giving it a squeeze. It wasn't meant to be sexual so much as intimate, and I'm shocked at the ease I feel around him already.

"So, what are you doing for Christmas?" he asks.

"Why? Want to spend it with me already?" I give him a cheeky smirk.

"I would love to spend it with you," he says and I almost

choke on my coffee. "I assume you're probably busy with your family though."

"Aren't you?"

"I usually work late Christmas Eve and early the day after Christmas so I'm too exhausted to travel to see extended family. My parents are going on a cruise this year."

"For Christmas? They aren't going to spend it with you?"

"I got it for them." He chuckles. "Honestly, sitting through a dinner with my parents and all my aunts badgering me about getting married gets old. I go visit my parents a few times a year in Florida, and trust me, that's enough." He laughs. "But don't worry about me." He taps my nose. "I usually go to Chris' house. He got divorced recently so we're going to be struggling a bit in the food department because his wife could cook, but I think we are just going to go out for dinner."

Part of me wants to invite them both but maybe that's crossing a line of boss-employee turned whatever this is. Besides Christmas has become my dad, Lucas, and my thing. We have traditions that are some of my favorite things of the year. My dad can't cook so we typically go out for Christmas Eve dinner and order in for Christmas Day. One year we attempted it ourselves which was an epic failure. We could have hired someone to come in to cook for us, but my dad likes it just being the three of us.

So now, we rotate different cuisines and order *that* in. This year, we decided on Indian food and I can't wait. We spend the day drinking eggnog and watching Christmas movies with the intermittent check-ins on whatever game is on. The three of us go on a walk at some point, which usually includes Avery from next door, and Christmas Day always ends with watching Home Alone where nine times out of ten I wake up at two in the morning to both Lucas and my dad asleep on their respective couches and the lights from the Christmas tree winking at me.

I'm not ready to bring someone into that, especially when I'm not sure what we even are. *But is that rude?*

No, you guys aren't anything. You had great sex once. Relax, Rae.

"We go out for Christmas Eve dinner and then order takeout for the day, so I get it." I laugh.

"You mentioned your dad and your brother, do you see your mom?" He asks and immediately I stiffen.

"Ummm...not usually. She lives in Europe."

"Oh. Really? Like full-time?"

"Since I was about sixteen, yeah. I don't think I've seen my mother on a holiday since my parents were married." I chuckle. "It's a complicated situation."

"You're not close?"

"Understatement of the century." His hand reaches for mine and immediately I feel safe and like opening up this part of myself to Wes may not hurt as much as it usually does. "When you're sixteen and your parents get divorced, you inevitably take sides. You may not mean to, but you typically gravitate towards one. Also, my mom was cheating on my dad, but that's not really my business. I learned that through eavesdropping. The important thing to note here is my dad was always the parent I could count on. He was there, he was present, he always showed up even when they were married." I sigh. "My mom ended up leaving my dad for the guy she was cheating on him with on Christmas Eve, and subsequently me and my brother because said guy didn't have a whole lot of interest in being a stepfather." I grimace. "This is the very short version, but yeah, Lucas and I were always so attached to our dad and this just didn't make it easier for us to have a great relationship with our mom."

Arms wrap around me and then I'm sitting in his lap. "I'm sorry, baby. That's really tough. I'm so sorry you went through something like that and at such an important age."

I shrug. "We got through it. The girl that lives next door, Avery? That's Lucas' best friend. But sometimes I got to borrow her and it was like I had a sister. Her and her mom would invite me sometimes when they did cute mother-daughter stuff and for a little while I could pretend I had one that cared." I don't say anything for a second and I remember I'm not talking to my therapist, or my best friend Natasha, or Lucas.

Fuck.

"Well, that got dark." I swallow. "Sorry." I had long stopped crying over my mommy issues so there weren't tears but I feel awkward and want off of his lap like *now.* I try to move when he grips me tighter and holds me against him. His hand reaches up behind my neck guiding my face to his, and then his lips are on mine, kissing me through my discomfort. I'm not into it at first but after a few swipes of his tongue against mine, I've changed my position so that I'm straddling him with my arms around his neck.

"I'm not sure why you're apologizing," he whispers against my lips before sliding his tongue against mine.

This man can kiss. Better than any guy I've ever kissed. He's done everything better than any guy. The way he touches me and kisses me and fucks me. *He made me squirt for God's sake.* A fact I'm not sure if I'm embarrassed about or not.

We are not embarrassed. Let him do it again! I practically hear my vagina scream at me.

I moan into his mouth as I continue to rock against him feeling my sex get slicker with every thrust against him. He pulls away, holding my face in his hands. "I'm sorry, I'm stopping. I'm seconds from fucking you on top of this bar and not only do I want you to finish eating, but I do have a little bit of work to do. Once we start, I know I'm not going to want to stop."

"Oh! Of course." I go to move off of him, and he holds me in place again.

"Give me an hour and then I'm all yours."

"Wes, I know you're busy. Don't worry about me. I can entertain myself." I wave him off because I meant it. I'm very familiar with a television and my cellphone. I'll be fine.

He grabs my face. "One hour. Trust me, I want to be all yours."

Chapter SIX

WES

I T ISN'T UNTIL THE NEXT MORNING THAT I TAKE RAEGAN home. I would have suggested she stay another day or even until we left for Miami a few days from now, but she said she needed to go home before her dad sent a search party. I'd heard the very watered-down version of her telling him she was staying at a friend's house and even though I knew why she told him that, I hate the thought of being labeled as only her friend.

I'm pulling into her neighborhood, her hand encased in mine and my eyes flit to her legs that are still in my sweatpants. I'd given her the smallest pair I still had from a pile of clothes I'm planning to donate so she wouldn't have to put on that tight skirt from the party. If it hadn't been a blizzard and I wasn't bringing her home today, I would have ordered some other clothes for her, but I'd be better prepared next time. I already contacted the woman who does my shopping that I needed some basic women's clothing. It may not be exactly what she wants, but at least it would be something she'd feel comfortable in while she was at my house. *Not that I minded seeing her in my clothes for two days.*

"I had fun." She looks at me and gives me a shy smile and I bring her hand to my mouth, to drag my lips over her knuckles.

"So did I." I want to tell her I want to do it again *and again.* But maybe she only wanted to do this once? *No, she made several comments alluding to this becoming a repeat occurrence.*

"I'll see you tomorrow," she says as I pull into her driveway. Her house looks warm and inviting and is decorated for Christmas with lights and a reindeer display in her front yard. Her eyes flit to the front door. "God, I hope my dad isn't at the window because I want to kiss you." She unbuckles her seatbelt and leans across the console presenting her lips. I take them eagerly, kissing her like I'll never see her again even though I know I'll see her tomorrow.

That feels like a lifetime though.

I cup her face as I kiss her, sliding my hands into her hair and tugging gently and she moans. I learned quickly that she loves when I play with her hair and I'm always rewarded with the sexiest sounds in response. "Are you sure I can't convince you to stay another night? You could go grab your clothes and come back with me." I drag my lips away from her mouth to place a kiss on her forehead and then her nose.

She sighs and when her eyes flutter open, I think she's considering it before her face changes and reality must set in. "And how would we explain showing up together tomorrow?" She raises an eyebrow at me and although we'd fucked three times this morning, I'm getting hard and I want her *again.*

"I'll bring you back in the morning for your car."

"That's silly." She presses another kiss to my lips and reaches for my door handle. "I'll see you tomorrow."

Say something. Anything that lets her know this isn't just sex. Tell her you want more than sex. NOW?

"I'll call you later," I blurt out.

Her head turns towards me and she gives me another one of those shy smiles. "Okay." She nods and gives me a final wave before she moves slowly towards her garage door and then she's gone.

"Well well well, look who finally decided to answer my call. I was about to show up at your house and pull you out from under her." Chris' voice floods my car when I finally return his calls. Despite the work I did yesterday, which mostly consisted of me pacing my office trying to will my dick down so I wouldn't go attack Raegan who I could hear giggling in my living room to an episode of *Friends,* I avoided Chris' calls, not wanting to get into it.

I roll my eyes. "I'm hanging up."

"Wait! So…"

"So what?"

"Don't so what, me. How was it? How was she? Did you confess your love for her? Please tell me you didn't actually propose?" He jokes referring to what he said at the party.

"How did you know I was with her?"

"You left and then shortly after she was nowhere to be found."

"Did anyone else notice that?"

"I don't think so," he says. "A lot of people left shortly after. Stop avoiding my questions."

"I didn't propose."

"Answer more of them."

"I didn't confess my love for her either."

"Jesus, Beck. Answer the good ones."

I groan in frustration, knowing he won't let this go. "It was the best sex of my life and that's all you're getting."

He whistles in response. "Well, I'm proud of you. It's been way too long since you've gotten laid. Almost a year now?"

"It irritates the shit out of me that you know that."

"Well, you've spent the last six months training your dick to only get hard for Raegan so, I can understand some of the reason behind your dry spell."

I want to argue with him but he's right. Since the moment she stepped into my office, my whole body has only responded to her.

"So, you've gotten it out of your system—" he starts and I frown.

"Far from that." I want to tell him I don't think I'll ever be able to get Raegan Graham out of my system but I know that's the quickest way to get a lecture I'm not in the mood for.

He's quiet for a second and then he sighs. "Wes."

"Oh, my first name." I chuckle. "Am I in trouble?"

"No. I mean…you just need to be careful."

"I will."

"Nothing on office grounds. No sneaking her into your office—"

"Not agreeing to any of that."

"Fuck. Man, you cannot. You're going to get caught."

"No, I won't."

"Yes. You fucking will. I know you and I also know what it looks like when you're into a woman. Although I've never seen you like this so early on. You weren't even like this when you started dating Hannah." A flair of annoyance shoots through me thinking about my ex-fiancée. While we parted somewhat amicably, we spent the majority of our final year together arguing about every single thing under the sun and forcing me back into therapy because I was so stressed out trying to keep things together at home and at work.

We were together for six years, the majority of my thirties before ending things about four years ago.

"Raegan is…different from Hannah."

"I'd fucking hope so. Hannah was the worst."

"Yes, I'm aware of your thoughts."

"Look, just be careful. Be cautious. And I don't know, jerk off before you come to work so you aren't so horned up you can't control yourself when you see her."

I want to tell him, it wouldn't matter if I jerked off, the second I see her, all bets are off. *I'm going to want my hands on her. My mouth on her. My dick inside her.*

I am so fucking screwed.

Later that night, after spending a day catching up on the work I blew off yesterday, I notice it's nearing ten o'clock. I'm barely out of my office before I have my phone to my ear to call Raegan. It rings a few times and I'm wondering if maybe it's too late and she's already asleep. I'm about to hang up when a sleepy voice comes over the line.

"Hey." Her voice already has the power to make my dick hard but this breathy and lethargically sexy voice she has, makes me wish I was crawling into bed next to her.

"Hey, beautiful. I'm sorry I'm calling you so late. Go back to sleep."

"No, I'm fine. I've slept a lot today." She chuckles. "We didn't do much sleeping."

I laugh as I start to shut off all the lights downstairs and turn the thermostat back down after Raegan had me turn it up to a few degrees above the temperature of hell. *We are going to need to talk about that.*

"I'll let you sleep a little more next time."

She yawns. "No, I doubt I'll ever want to waste a minute sleeping when I'm with you." I grab my dick, trying to get it to stay down so I don't suggest phone sex when she lets out a sexy little sigh. "I wish you were here." I hear her inhale lightly. "I've been smelling your shirt I stole all day. It smells like you."

"And you left me with nothing."

"I had nothing to leave you! I came to your house with the clothes on my back and my purse." She giggles.

"You absolutely had something you could have left me. That tiny piece of fabric that sits against your cunt."

"Next time."

"Bring me a pair tomorrow."

She gasps. "Wes, we need to behave at work."

What is everyone's deal about that? "We'll see."

"We don't want to get caught."

"We won't and I vividly remember you saying I could eat your pussy in my office during my conference call."

"I knew that was going to come back to bite me in the ass," she mumbles. "Wes, I was so drunk on you I would have agreed to fucking on the conference room table during one of your board meetings."

"Oh, so you lied to me?" I tease.

"No, I was just…horny, and everything just felt so good."

"It certainly did." I pull my dick thinking about this weekend for the hundredth time. "Are you wearing my sweatpants?"

"Mmhmm."

"So, you're wearing all my clothes?"

"Yes."

"Are you wearing panties?"

"No."

"Fuck." I growl thinking about my sweatpants resting against her pretty cunt. "I wish *you* were here."

"So...I know we have to leave early Wednesday." She clears her throat. "Maybe I should stay over Tuesday night?"

"Yes," I answer immediately. "I'll send you the codes to get into my house so you can come over right from work. I'll probably be working a little late."

"Oh, I can wait until you get home—"

"No. Come here," I interrupt her. "It'll keep me focused knowing you'll be here when I get home."

"Okay." And I can hear the smile in her voice. "I'll probably go home first to drop off my car and take an Uber."

"I'll send a car to pick you up."

"That's not necessary," she argues.

"It's very necessary. You'd expense an Uber anyway, why wouldn't I send a car with a driver I actually know and trust?"

"You're very bossy," she says. "I think you're bossier now than you were before."

"You can boss me around too, you know," I tell her.

"Oh?"

I'm sitting on the couch in my room that Raegan and I somehow managed to sixty-nine on and I smile at the memory. "I recall you being quite bossy in bed if I recall."

"I am not!" She says and I can almost see the smirk on those full lips because she knows she is.

"Come to my office when you get in tomorrow," I tell her, switching the conversation to what I really want to talk about, which is how soon can I see her face.

"Wes, we need to be somewhat professional."

A smile pulls at my lips. "Well, you can bring me a coffee if you'd like."

"Are you ordering me to bring you a coffee?" I hear the cheekiness in her voice.

"If that's the only way to get you into my office first thing tomorrow, then yes."

"Fine. Coffee tomorrow, but you need to behave."

We'll see.

The light knocking on my office door already makes me feel better after the shitshow that's been the last hour. It is barely eight in the morning and I've already been successfully pissed off more than once. "Come in," I call out and it takes a few moments for my entire body to register that Raegan is not walking through the door. *What the fuck?*

In walks Nigel Samuels, this annoying fucker from marketing who is always trying to get me to attend more events.

"Hi, Mr. Beckham." *For the love of God, I am not in the mood.* "I'm just here to go over your itinerary for Miami."

"Must we do this now?" I shoot him a look I know he's more than familiar with.

"Yes," he says and I'll admit, though he annoys the shit out of me, he's one of few people that stands up to me. It's impressive even if he is irritating as hell. "You need to go to at least one of the events I sent. I also heard you're going down on Wednesday now? There's something that night—"

"No," I tell him because the only thing I plan on doing Wednesday night is eating Raegan's pussy.

"It's just a gallery opening. Super lowkey, you can be in and out," he says without looking up from his iPad. "They're a decent client, Wes."

I think about it, wondering if maybe it's something Raegan would want to do with me.

Like a date?

"Fine. RSVP yes for me, plus one," I tell him. "My assistant is going down a day early as well." It isn't unheard of for any of our assistants to go with us anywhere so Nigel doesn't even bat an eye.

"Wonderful, I'll do this now. Now, Thursday—" he starts when there's another knock on the door.

"I'll look it over and email you back," I tell him. "Come in," I say as I make my way towards the door, praying that it's Raegan this time. My prayers are answered when I see her peek her head in and give me a sweet smile before her gaze sweeps to Nigel on my couch.

"Mr. Beckham, I have your coffee and I have a few messages for you, but I can come back if you're busy."

"Not necessary. Nigel was just leaving." I open the door wider and usher her in before taking the coffee from her hands. "Thank you." I try not to let my gaze linger on her while Nigel is in the room but she's wearing a gray pencil skirt that highlights her waist and her gorgeous legs and now I'm picturing them wrapped around my waist…or my neck.

"I want an answer by the end of the day," he says and I scoff in response.

"You'll get an answer when you get an answer," I say as I close the door before he can respond.

I turn around, keeping my back against the door as I drag my eyes up Raegan's body, slowly, relishing in the fact that we are alone and I can openly stare at her.

"Hey." She smiles when my eyes reach hers.

"Hey." I hold up the lidded paper cup. "Thank you for the

coffee." I push off the door and make my way towards her my smile getting wider with every step I get closer to her. "And for letting me see this face." I cup her chin and tilt it upwards.

"We are supposed to be behaving," she whispers just before my lips brush against hers.

"I am behaving. I could have my hand up your skirt."

She bites her bottom lip and looks at the door behind me then back to me, and I can almost hear her thinking about whether we could misbehave a *little*. I'm about to suggest that when my door opens and Chris walks in with his phone pressed to his ear. I take a step back from Raegan and Chris looks at us with a shit-eating grin. I can sense the nerves flowing off of Raegan and I want to tell her that it's fine and that Chris already knows.

Even though I told her she couldn't tell anyone.

"Let me call you back," he says before he closes the door behind him.

"Forget how to knock?" I ask him with a glare.

"Excuse me for not expecting you to be busy when we have a meeting in two minutes with Jason from the sales team."

"Fuck." I grit out. "Miss Graham, can you hold my calls for the next hour and please shut my door on your way out?" She nods once before she's out the door without another look at me.

I'd only barely brushed my lips against hers when I'd fully planned to kiss her senseless when I saw her.

"Fifteen whole minutes," Chris says, looking at his watch. "That's got to be a record."

"Don't bust my balls."

"HR will cut them off if they find out."

"They're not going to if you keep your mouth shut and don't walk into my office without knocking."

Chapter SEVEN

Raegan

THE FOLLOWING DAY I'M SITTING AT MY DESK WHEN I hear Marissa from behind me. "So, what time are you getting to the airport on Thursday? I'm considering getting there a little early to get a mimosa or a shot or something to get a nice buzz before the flight."

I hadn't told anyone I was flying to Miami a day early with Wes, not because I was hiding it, but because it hadn't come up. We'd had a meeting yesterday regarding our trip and Wes hadn't mentioned that we'd be going a day early, so I'm not sure if it's a secret or if he just wants to keep people—*namely Chris*—out of his business. I have a sneaking suspicion that he knows what is going on.

I'd been able to get away with my Irish exit from the holiday party because Marissa was pretty drunk, but she'd definitely pressed the question of whether anything happened between Wes and me. I'd told her I suddenly wasn't feeling well and I went home. Luckily, she seemed to buy it.

I spin around in my chair to face her and she's already facing me. "Oh, I'm actually going down tomorrow."

She takes a sip of her coffee and cocks her head to the side. "What? Why?"

"Because Wes decided to go a day early."

She raises an eyebrow at me and glides across our cubicle in her chair. "Oh *really*? Did he ask you to come?"

"No...not exactly. He gave me the option."

"And you took it?" She leans on my desk and purses her lips as she tucks a dark curly strand behind her ear. "Oh. My. God." She taps my nose with each word. "You're going down to Miami early *alone* with our boss that has a major crush on you." She squeals. "Did you wax?"

Yes.

"Marissa, I love this imagination you have but I really don't think he has a crush on me." My nipples tingling in my shirt refute that claim. *Just the thought of him makes them hard.*

"You're so full of shit. You know he does! Oh my gosh, you're going to get to the hotel and something is going to happen with one of your rooms forcing you into a room together with only *one* bed." She giggles. "If he offers to sleep on the couch or the floor or some gentlemanly bullshit you say no. Do you understand me? NO. I hope you're planning to take some sexy pajamas."

Yes again.

I chuckle. "You and your romance novels."

"I'm serious! Look, this is the perfect time. I'll bet he takes you on a date." She squeals again and rolls back to her side of the cubicle.

I'm about to respond when my phone rings and I see

the number I've spent about half the day waiting for. "Hi, Mr. Beckham."

"Take your panties off and come to my office." I hear his voice low in my ear and I press a hand to my mouth to stop the moan that is threatening to escape.

"Is this time sensitive?"

"Yes. I need to touch you." We had a very horny and sexy round of phone sex last night, but we haven't really touched each other in two days and I'm guessing he's feeling just as needy as I am. We should really wait until tonight. I'm already packed and ready for Miami, and I'm glad we decided that I would stay over tonight because I want several repeats of what happened over the weekend.

"Right, okay. I'll be right there." I'm out of my chair and my cubicle, grateful that Marissa is now on a call as I walk to the bathroom.

I enter the stall and slide my panties down my legs, grateful that I'm wearing thigh-highs to make this process much easier. I'll admit I've been purposely wearing these instead of full pantyhose in case Wes was able to wear me down. I look down at my pussy, already wet and glistening just from the two sentences he said to me on the phone, and slide my panties into my blazer pocket. I let out a long breath as the air tickles the wet flesh before exiting the stall to wash my hands.

I'm walking towards Wes' office when I hear my name being called and Liam is walking towards me.

Fuck, this is not what I need.

"Hey, I'm actually on my way to Mr. Beckham's office."

"Oh great, I'll walk with you. I'm headed there anyway," he responds. With every step towards his office, my sex gets wetter and I'm trying not to focus on that.

"So, where did you disappear to at the holiday party? It was like one minute you were there and the next you weren't," Liam says, his face filled with concern.

"Oh, I went home. I wasn't feeling well."

As we get closer to Wes' office, I can already imagine his irritation at us walking in together. *Or maybe I'm sensing my own irritation?*

"I wish you would have told me; I could have taken you home so you didn't have to Uber." He smiles and I nod.

"Right." Now, I'm suddenly nervous because what if he can smell my arousal?

No, you're being paranoid.

I move, putting more space between us as we continue walking. "So, do you need a ride to the airport on Thursday or are you going with Marissa?"

"Oh…no I'm actually going tomorrow."

He stops walking and furrows his brows, giving me a look of confusion and maybe also disappointment like he knows why I would be flying down early alone with our boss. *But no, this was decided before we did anything. Not that it's his business.*

"Why?"

I stop walking even though I really don't want to. "Mr. Beckham is and I'm his assistant."

He slides his hands into his pockets. "You know you don't have to."

I cross my arms over my chest, not to be combative but because I'm actually a little nervous. "Of course, he gave me a choice."

Liam nods and looks towards Wes' door and then back to me. "Look Raegan, I know it's easy to get caught up with someone like him. I've seen girls become enamored with him and it never works out well."

I'm not exactly sure what he's trying to say here but I don't love the implication.

"Liam, I'm not one to beat around the bush. What are you saying?"

"I'm saying I would hate to see you get hurt or even fired for getting involved with someone you shouldn't. The things I've heard about him and Holt both..." he says.

I try not to show the sting I feel because what has he heard? Wes said he'd never been attracted to anyone he worked for which I assume would mean he's never touched anyone.

"You can't believe everything you hear."

"But I believe everything I *see*, Rae. And so should you. Women throw themselves at him. Do you want to be that kind of woman?"

Now, I'm annoyed. "You're giving me whiplash and it's a little irritating. Either you think I'm throwing myself at him or that we are doing something that could get me fired. Both are insulting by the way, but by all means, pick one."

He sighs, probably not happy with the fact that he's not getting the results he wants in this conversation. "It's all under the same umbrella—" he says just as the door a few feet ahead opens and Wes strides out.

I already know he's looking for me and he hides his look of shock well when he sees me just a few feet from his door. The look of annoyance however spreads when he sees who I'm talking to. "Miss Graham, when I ask for you to come to my office, I don't expect you to stop to chat." My cheeks turn pink and I resist the urge to glare at him because I'm already annoyed with Liam, and he's making it worse.

"My apologies," I say, wanting to throw Liam under the bus but deciding against it.

"And Mr. Patterson, do you have something else to do besides bother my assistant while she's working?"

"I was actually on my way to your office." His voice is direct, almost condescending and I really hope this doesn't turn into some sort of pissing contest.

"Very well, let's go." He looks at Liam before turning to me. "I'll buzz you when I'm finished," he says before turning and walking away with Liam.

Fifteen minutes later my phone rings again, and before I can even utter a greeting I hear his voice, hard and urgent. "My office and do not talk to anyone unless you want me to fire them."

I hang up the phone without responding and I make my way to his office.

"Come in," I hear after I knock lightly, and when I open the door, he's standing directly in front of it. His glasses are off and he looks like he's about to lose it. I close the door behind me and then his lips are on mine, kissing me hard and deep. His tongue dances with mine and I moan against his mouth. *I will never get over how well this man kisses.* He cups my face before pushing his hands into my hair. I wrap my arms around his neck and play with the hair at the nape of his neck as I try to push myself closer to him.

"Wes," I whisper against his mouth.

"I love the way my name sounds on your lips." He pulls his lips away from mine and when my eyes flutter open, he's staring at me like he can't believe I'm in front of him. "Hi, beautiful."

"Hey." I smile and I know I've got a dreamy look on my face.

"It's been too long since I've kissed you," he says as he rubs my lips. "Here." He drags his hand down between my legs and up my skirt. "Or here." He groans at the same second I gasp when his fingers hit my wet clit. "Fuck, you took your panties off," he says as he continues to run his fingers through my slit.

"Of course, you told me to."

"Did you talk to that tool with no panties on?"

"I was on my way to your office." I moan just as he moves away from my clit and pushes two fingers inside me.

"What did he say to you?"

"I...can I come first?" I bat my eyelashes at him.

"It's going to piss me off, isn't it?"

"Probably."

"Fuck." He pulls his fingers out of me and takes a step back as he reaches for my hand and drags me across his office towards the windows.

He spins me around to face the window and presses his chest against my back. He moves my hair to one side and presses his lips to my neck as he hikes my skirt up to my hips.

"I'm sorry I was short with you by the way."

The sincerity in his voice makes my heart flutter in my chest. "I get it."

"Still." He licks a trail up my neck. "I wouldn't have if he wasn't standing there. Now tell me what he said."

I moan as his fingers move back to my clit, rubbing it gently and causing my entire body to sizzle. "I don't want you to be angry."

"I'd never be angry with you."

"I didn't mean with me."

"Well, he needs to mind his own fucking business and then I wouldn't have a reason to be."

"He just...kind of warned me about getting involved with you so I don't get fired."

"Yeah, I'll bet. It's obvious as hell that he wants in your panties, baby." He rubs my clit harder and I can feel his dick against my back. *And now I'm thinking about that delicious piercing.*

I reach into my pocket and pull my panties out, letting them dangle from my index finger. They're red and silk and a little wet and I can hear his breathing change in my ear the second he sees them. "Well, that will be pretty difficult considering you have them."

He chuckles in my ear and I'm happy that I've been able

to calm him. He takes them from my hand and I hear a deep inhale. When I turn my head, I see them under his nose before he pockets them. "God, you smell so good." I can hear the resolve in his voice withering. "How do you want to come?" He's rubbing me softer now, like he just wants to keep me on the edge but not enough to push me over.

I let my head fall back against him. "I have a choice?"

"Yes, Angel, you can come like this or on my tongue or…"

His piercing comes to mind and before I can tell myself that riding Wes' dick in his office is not a good idea, I've turned around, removing his hand from between my legs. "Or?" I look down and am already unbuckling his belt before I say it. "Around your dick?"

When I look up his blue eyes are hooded. "Mmmhm."

I lick my lips and drop to my knees instantly, pulling his pants and briefs down together and practically drooling when his dick comes into view. *How did I forget how pretty it is?* "I want this." I run my tongue up and down the shaft, swirling my tongue around the tip, paying much attention to his piercings.

"Oh fuck, me too, baby."

I stand up and move to his desk, hopping up on it and spreading my legs obscenely for him. "Come here."

"See." He smiles. *"Bossy."*

"You like it." I smirk just as he holds his dick to my cunt, rubbing the tip of it against my clit.

"You bet I do." He looks behind me towards the door. "You know you have to be quiet."

I nod and send him a cheeky grin. "I'm surprised you don't want every man on the floor to know that only your dick can make me come."

I feel his dick twitch against my clit and I bite my bottom lip to stifle a moan. "If it wasn't against the rules, you bet your ass I would." He pulls my body so my ass is on the edge of the desk and pushes into me. "Fuck," he whispers and I already feel him pulsing inside of me.

"Shit," I whisper. "Condom." He goes to pull out when I wrap my legs around him, preventing him from moving. "Wait."

His eyes stare down at me curiously and I'm not even sure what to say because while I did request a refill of my birth control prescription I used to take, I haven't started taking it yet. *I also haven't told him this yet.*

"Whatever you want." He's still inside of me, his arms wrapped around me, and his blue eyes so full of warmth and sincerity and something I've never seen in a man's eyes before.

"Can you pull out?"

"Of course." I look down at my body which still has my white blouse tucked into my skirt that's bunched up and look around at where he could come. "In here." His hand finds my mouth and squeezes my jaw.

I nod. "Make sure you leave enough time for me to get off the desk." I giggle and he smiles before he pushes his lips to mine and begins fucking me again. He does it slowly, so as not to make noise. We aren't even kissing like we used to, loud and wet and sexy. It's slow and sensual and dare I say, more intimate.

"Oh fuck, Raegan. You are so incredible. Do you know how much I want you?" He groans low in my ear and the way he's trying to pace his thrusts from getting too frantic leads me to believe he may be closer than I am.

I pull away from his mouth and his eyes pop open. "Are you about to come?"

"I can hold it," he says through gritted teeth and I frown.

"No." I try to push him off when he keeps us pinned together.

"Honey, I need you to come on my dick first."

"But you're fighting it, I can come on your dick later. I'd rather you not accidentally come inside me."

He shakes his head as a frown crosses his face. "I would never do something you didn't want."

"I know you wouldn't on purpose."

"I'm forty-one, Raegan, I know how to hold off on coming."

The reminder of his age sends a shiver through me. "Sounds like I'm not doing my job right." I raise an eyebrow at him before I push him off with a little more force and drop to my knees, sheathing my mouth around him.

"Oh, fuck me, Raegan. You are definitely doing your job right; is that what you want to hear?" He runs a hand through my hair. "You know my dick better than anyone ever has after three fucking days." He groans. "Baby, I want to fuck your mouth."

I let him fall out momentarily. "Yes *please*," I say and then his hands are on both sides of my head as he pushes his dick as far as it can go, tapping the back of my throat. It only takes three strokes before he's exploding down my throat and when I look up, his head is thrown back with a hand over his face. I barely have a chance to swallow before I'm hauled to my feet, placed back on his desk, and he drops to his knees before lowering his face to my sex.

"Wes," I moan quietly, proud of myself for being able to stifle my sounds. "I am going to scream your house down later."

"Fuck yeah you are." He growls against me. My pussy is still sensitive from when he was inside of me and I can already feel the familiar tingle of an orgasm brewing at my toes. He is lapping at me slowly, giving me long strokes from my entrance to the top of my mound before flicking my clit and swirling his tongue around it.

"Oh God." I lower my gaze and see him looking right at me, his eyes hungry and sexy. "I—I'm going to come." I let out several shaky breaths and bite my bottom lip to keep from moaning just as I go over the edge. I throw my head back, riding out the rest of my climax all over his tongue. When I stop coming, he stands in front of me, his lips shiny and wet from my pussy.

"I can't wait to do this again when I get you home." He presses his lips to mine gently and I taste myself on his mouth. "I want to hear all the sexy things you say when you're about to come." I rub my bottom lip, wiping myself from the skin. "Don't you taste good? I would eat you all day if I could."

"No one has ever kissed me after they did…*that*."

"Oh?" He grins revealing that dimple that makes me weak in the knees. "You want a better taste?" I blink at him wondering what he means but knowing I trust him so I nod slowly. He's back at my entrance again, licking me all over. "Wes, I can't again," I whisper. His tongue moves inside of me and swirls around my opening before dragging through my slit again. Then he's back in front of me and grips my jaw making my mouth pop open and lets his mouth hover over mine letting me know what he's planning to do. My eyes widen but I nod again and he lets a stream of spit fall into my mouth.

Oh. My. God. That's the hottest thing anyone's ever done to me. He closes my mouth and drops a kiss on my lips. "Wow. I—" I swallow before letting out a breath and look around the room. "That was so hot."

"*You* are so hot, Raegan." He rubs his nose against mine and then pulls me off the desk into his arms as he pushes my skirt down. "Was that last part okay?" He pulls away to look at me, placing his hands on my shoulders.

"Yes. I loved that…it was hot and kind of dirty." I look up at him and the look he's giving me makes me want to mount him right now. "What are you doing to me, Wes Beckham?" I ask as I fix my skirt.

"The same thing you're doing to me."

Chapter EIGHT

WES

IT'S ALMOST NINE-THIRTY BY THE TIME I GET HOME, AND just as I thought, knowing that Raegan was at my house had me laser-focused.

"Raegan?" I call for her as soon as I enter my kitchen and see that she cooked something *and* baked something? I spot some sort of pasta and brownies and I can't remember the last time I've come home from work to dinner being made for me. I put my laptop bag and briefcase on the island and go in search of Raegan hoping she's not asleep. I would feel like shit for waking her up, but I'm fucking desperate for her. I see her shoes by the door and I can't help the rush that comes with the thought of her being here all the time.

I move up the stairs and when I enter my room, I hear my shower running. I shed my clothes with each step towards the bathroom knowing I'm about to see Raegan wet and naked and

I'm already hard. I enter the bathroom and watch her through the glass. Her back is to me and I don't want to scare her by just opening the door so I clear my throat.

She turns around slowly and wipes a hand against the foggy glass and the smile that crosses her face is so fucking sexy. She pushes the door open and looks down at my naked form.

"I thought I could be in and out before you got home." She bites her bottom lip as I move towards her, her eyes trained on my dick. "But this is better."

"Damn right, it is," I tell her as the door closes behind me and she's in my arms instantly like our bodies are magnets. "You cooked?"

"Just some penne pasta with meat sauce. Nothing fancy, but I thought you may be hungry," she giggles, "and okay, I was hungry. I know it's a little late now, but I thought you'd be here a little earlier."

"Thank you," I tell her between kisses. "I am hungry, and after I eat *you*, I'll eat." I press my lips to hers, pushing my hands through her wet hair as I devour her mouth more aggressively than I did in my office today while I was trying to be quiet. I trail my lips down her neck and chest and immediately suck one of her tits into my mouth. I roll the nipple around my tongue sucking and pulling it and running my teeth over it gently. "I fucking love your pretty tits." When I hear a whine above my head I move to the other, giving it the same attention. Then, I feel her hands on my cheeks and her gently pulling me off her breasts.

"I saw the clothes you got for me." She pulls back and looks up at me. Her eyes are completely free of makeup and I note that they're a little glassy. I'm not sure if it's due to emotion or the water from the shower. "That was really sweet. Thank you."

Her gratefulness tugs at my heart, especially since I'm sure she's used to getting whatever she wants or needs without batting an eye. "I hated that you didn't have anything here last weekend." I glide my hands up her wet body. She smells like peppermint and I note the body wash behind her.

"I did love being in your clothes though," she purrs.

I press my nose to her neck and inhale. *Fuck, she smells good.* "And you can still wear my clothes. Anything you want. But at least now you have some options."

"Wes…" She takes a step back and puts her hands on her hips, her eyes not on me, and I can see her mind working.

"What, baby? Talk to me." I put my hands on her shoulders before dragging them up her neck to her face and turning her chin gently to face me.

"I feel like we are moving really fast, or maybe I'm overthinking it and you just want to be casual. Do you want to be casual?" The words come out in a rush. "Fuck, I shouldn't have said that."

"Yes, you should have. Don't feel like you have to hide anything from me. Quite frankly, I'm glad you said something because I want to know what's going on up here." I tap her temple. "Let me be very clear, so there's no confusion. I do *not* want to be casual." I drag my hands away from her face and down her body to her ass and lift her into my arms. Her legs wrap around my waist and she locks her ankles around my back. "I'm only sleeping with you. You're the only woman who has the codes to my house. I spend about half of my days thinking about you and the rest of the time you're sitting in the back of my mind waiting for a free moment to come back to the front. I am consumed by *you,* Raegan. You say it's fast…but that's just for *you.* I've been here for about six months. You're just catching up."

She gasps and I continue, hoping to drive home the part that I want her and only her. "So, we have some plans for tomorrow night in Miami. I have to go to this gallery opening but I want to be in and out and then I was hoping you'd like to have dinner."

"Are you asking me on a date?" Her tone is hopeful and I see the excitement in her eyes.

"Yes." She presses her lips to mine and then I feel her hands between us feeling for my dick and then I'm inside of her. "Is that a yes?" I groan low in her ear as I begin thrusting inside of her.

"I would say something smart but I don't want you to stop." She chuckles and then lets out a moan as she lets her head fall back against the tile. "It's a yes." I pin her to the shower wall and look down between us where my dick is completely inside of her. Her cunt is stretched around me and my pubic hair is pressed directly against her mound. It is fucking sexy and erotic and I want this image ingrained in my brain forever.

"Wes. Oh…God." She moans. "Right there." I grip her hips pulling her harder and faster on my dick, digging my nails into her skin.

"Yeah? That feel good?"

"Yes yes yes." She cries just as her hand snakes down between us to rub her clit. "Fuck, I'm going to come all over your dick."

My dick throbs inside of her, wanting to come with her. "Is that right? After you said you couldn't?"

"It's because I didn't have the right dick inside of me." She drags her fingertips up my torso and wraps her arms around my neck as she begins to move her body up and down my stiff cock. "But I should have known you'd be different after months of my nipples tingling the second you walked in a room."

I grip her jaw to make her look at me. "Every time?"

"They'd actually ache sometimes when you looked at me."

"Fuck."

Her eyes look down before gliding up my body to meet my eyes and they're so intense and filled with lust. "Wes, I think I've wanted you for just as long as you've wanted me, I just didn't think…this was possible so I tried to ignore it." I stop thrusting but remain inside of her, my dick still pulsing. "I think I'm caught up now," she whispers and then I pull her away from the wall, keeping my dick still inside of her as I walk to the built-in bench in my shower. I sit down with her in my lap and lean back.

"Ride me, baby. Make yourself come all over me."

"Are you very close?" she asks.

"I'm fine," I tell her because nothing matters more than getting her off.

"Can I play with your piercings?"

I groan because I'm not exactly *that fine.* I swallow. "For a second."

She giggles as she pulls my dick out of her and holds it against her sex. "Is this hard for you?"

"Hard to watch, hard to feel. You're rubbing my dick against your clit until you come all over it while making these sexy little noises and rubbing my balls at the same time. Yes, Angel, it's hard not to come."

"Pretty soon you won't have to worry about it." She gasps as she rolls her clit over the metal and right on time one of her hands reaches behind her to rub my balls.

I tilt her chin upwards to look at me. "What was that?"

"I refilled my prescription to go back on the pill…so we don't have to be *so* careful," she purrs.

"Fuuuuuck. You tell me this now?" My dick hardens just as she spins her hips in a circle and lets out a moan.

"I—wanted to surprise you. I want to feel you come inside of me." She bites her bottom lip. "We probably shouldn't every time but I'd like to feel it sometimes."

Fuck, all of this talk about me fucking her raw and coming inside of her all while she's using my cock to masturbate is not fucking helping.

"Honey, I need you to stop. I'm going to—" My eyes slam shut and just as I feel the tip of my dick rub against that tiny bundle of nerves for the hundredth time, I feel my climax shoot through me. "Oh, fuck fuck fuck, baby, yes right fucking there." I growl as I reach for my dick, feeling her hand still wrapped around it. I wrap my hand around hers as we both wring the rest of my orgasm out. She's still sitting on my thighs so I can only hope she moved slightly out of the way so I didn't cover her very unprotected cunt with my orgasm.

"Oh my God. Yes." She moans and when I finally open my eyes, she's still rubbing my dick against her, her pussy covered in a layer of *me*. "I'm going to come, oh fuck." She grabs my dick that's starting to soften and I watch in fascination as her orgasm washes over her as she spasms and climaxes all over my dick. "Wes!" She squeals and a breathy moan or laugh leaves her lips.

Fuck, she looks sexy as hell.

Her eyes flutter open and they immediately look down and then at me. Our eyes lock for no more than a second before she moves off of me and I'm behind her, helping her wash my cum off of her. "That was…hot," she says. "And risky." She bites her bottom lip and I see the pink on her cheeks. "I'm sorry."

She's sorry? For what? "What are you sorry for?"

"Not stopping when you told me to."

"Yes, we will need to work on your listening skills." I give her a look of mock scolding. "I love seeing my cum on you." I continue rinsing her off and hold the showerhead against her pussy.

"Wes," she moans.

"Raegan."

"Can we get out? You should eat and then I want to ride your face."

The next morning, I wake up to the very early alarm I set so Raegan and I would have time to fool around before we left for the airport. It's four in the morning so my room is still pitch black and I feel Raegan's weight on top of me. Even after five days and only sleeping in the same bed for three of them, our bodies are like magnets in our sleep. I feel her cheek on my chest, her hand on my shoulder, and she's got a leg between mine letting my dick rest against her thigh. My hand is resting on her lower back and I move us gently so she's on her back and I'm hovering on top of her.

I'm already hard, probably from the last five hours of her grinding on me and my dick subconsciously in her sleep. She's still wet, from me going down on her before she fell asleep so I glide against her slippery clit a few times before pushing inside. "Wake up, baby." I press a kiss to her neck and then her chest. Even in the dark, I know every part of her like we've been doing this for years.

"Mmmm, it's so dark," she whispers. "This feels like a dream."

"You dream about me fucking you?" I press my lips to hers and her arms wrap around me.

"Yes," she moans as I spin my hips in a circle doing my best to stimulate her clit.

"What happens in these dreams?"

"You pull me over your knee and spank me." My cock jerks at her words and she gasps at how deep I go. "And then you bend me over your desk and fuck me from behind with my ass bright red from your handprint."

Well, I was certainly not expecting that confession at four in the morning. "Holy fuck, Raegan, are you trying to kill me?" I keep rocking in and out of her slowly as I find her hands, lacing our fingers together, and pull them to hold above her head. "What else?"

"I was thinking..." She lets out a sigh that makes the throb in my dick pound faster. "Well, hoping...you'd fuck me on the plane later?"

"Fuck yes, I already planned that."

"I also think..." *Fuck there's more? I don't think my dick can take much more of her fantasy confessions.* "I may have a little bit of a daddy kink."

I'm out of her in an instant, my climax missing the inside of her cunt by a second as I come all over her stomach. I grab my dick, jerking it from root to tip over and over, wishing I was draining it inside of her while she screamed that D word.

Fuck. I am in so deep with this girl.

I reach for the side lamp on my nightstand and turn it on, and I'm grateful for my aim even in the dark. It's only on her stomach and tits and a few drops on her lips that she's wiping off and pushing into her mouth with a smirk. "My plan was to make you come first." I chuckle as I slide on my glasses and get off the bed to get a washcloth. "My plan is always to make you come first and then you derail it with your dirty talk."

She doesn't say anything as I move back into the room and begin to clean her off. She watches me intently and when I'm done, she sits up. Her eyes don't meet mine and I turn her face to me, wanting those pretty blue eyes on me. I give her a look that she must understand because she sighs.

"I can't believe I said all of that." She draws her legs up to her chin and hugs them before pressing her forehead to her knees.

"Wait." I move to sit next to her and pull her into my lap so she's facing me. Her cheeks are pink and she's still trying to avoid my gaze so I hold her face steady.

"Can we turn the lights back off?"

"No. Honey, spanking and sex on a plane and calling me daddy in bed? What are you thinking? That you turned me off? Did you see how hard and fast I came?" I know she's a bit naive but I want to tell her there's an entire world of kinky things out there for us to try and this is just the tip of the iceberg.

"Well, maybe not so much the first two…" She moves a little closer to me and I'm happy that she's feeling more comfortable because I felt her discomfort in my veins and I didn't like it. I wrap my arms around her and she snuggles into my neck. "I've never thought I would be into it and then Marissa said something in passing and I just haven't been able to get it out of my head."

I'm staring down at my phone reading an email when Raegan walks into the kitchen in a black dress that comes to just above her knees with a white blouse underneath it and black heels that I'm already picturing wrapped around my waist as I slip inside of her. She looks sexy as hell while still professional and I'm already annoyed at the thought of anyone hitting on her the second we get to Miami. "You look beautiful."

"Thank you." She beams before letting her eyes rove over me suggestively. My body responds to her instantly and I have to look away from her sexy blue eyes that already have the power to disarm me for a second. Otherwise, I'll have us both naked and her underneath me.

"Don't look at me like that, we don't have time."

"Like what?" Her eyes drop to my groin and she moves a little closer to me.

I take a step back. "Raegan," I warn her and she bites down

on her bottom lip just as she presses her body right up against mine and gently pulls my cup from my hand.

"Yes?" She tilts the mug towards her mouth and takes a sip without breaking our gaze and I'm instantly enthralled by her mouth and that tongue that glides across her bottom lip after she swallows.

"You're being a tease."

"Am I?" She sighs before she straightens my tie and drags her fingertips slowly down my chest. "You look nice."

I clear my throat, trying to ignore the rising in my slacks but she's pushing me. "Once we're on the plane," I say reluctantly through gritted teeth because those are absolutely not the words I want to be uttering. "We have to go. The car is outside."

The ride to the airport is mostly quiet. As much as I wanted to spend it with her in my lap, I needed to answer some emails and call Chris, who was unfortunately now flying down tonight and seemed to want to join Raegan and me for dinner. *Hard pass.*

Even though we didn't say much, she reached for my hand the second we got in the car and I didn't let it go the entire ride. It felt natural and easy despite the mountain of complications we have between us.

When we arrive at the private airport I fly out of, we walk to the private jet, our hands still laced as one of our flight attendants rolls our suitcases behind us. We make it up the boarding stairs and I'm pleased to see all of the things I requested already in place. There is a bottle of champagne placed in a bucket, an array of breakfast foods laid out on the table along with a bouquet of red roses. There are two creamy beige seats facing front that recline and matching couches directly behind it that line the plane back to the master bedroom and bathroom where Raegan and I will be the second we get to twenty thousand feet. There's also a dining area just before the bedroom with a television that currently has a fireplace ambiance displayed on the screen.

"Wow, this is incredible." She turns around to face me. "Does everyone take this jet?" She narrows her eyes. "Seems a little intimate."

"No, this is just for me or Chris when he wants to use it. The *Beckham Securities* jet is the same size but without the master bedroom in the back. Give me one second; I'm just going to go talk to the pilot and the crew." I pull her into my arms and place a kiss on her lips. "Make yourself comfortable."

Chapter NINE

Raegan

OH, MY GOD. MY EYES TAKE IN EVERY INCH OF THIS very luxurious private jet. I've been on private jets before but never like *this.* This screams wealth and glamour and…sex. I wasn't exaggerating when I said it felt too intimate for a company jet and I was glad to know he didn't usually have multiple people in this flying aphrodisiac. The second I stepped on the plane, I wanted him. *Is it too early for champagne?* I let out a breath as my nerves that sometimes pop up when I'm preparing to fly start to creep into my senses. Coupled with my nerves regarding the man who is also slowly starting to creep into my heart, I think I need a drink even though the sun has barely started to rise.

I walk towards the room in the back of the plane and am stunned to see a full-sized bedroom complete with a king-sized bed, another television, a closet, and a small dresser. Straight ahead is a wall of glass where I spy a bathtub and a shower, so anyone in the bedroom could watch someone showering or taking a bath. I put my purse on the bed and sit down next to it, sliding my heels off and immediately spot two sets of slippers next to the bed. I slide them on and walk back into the main cabin to see Wes pouring a glass of champagne and I briefly wonder if I'd said that out loud.

"Hey." He smiles and hands me a glass. "I was going to bring this to you. We are going to be taking off soon. They do like us to be seated before but once we are in the air we can go back there." He nods, giving me a wicked smirk. "Did you see the bathroom?"

"Yes, so cool. This is definitely the nicest private jet I've ever been on." I grab the glass of champagne and sit in the seat on one side of the aisle as he sits in the other. We are far enough apart that he can't hold my hand and suddenly a wave of nerves hits me when I realize that I've never been on a plane let alone a private jet without my dad or my brother or my friends from college when we took trips for spring break. When I've flown on private jets before, it was usually when I was a kid *without a care in the world,* with the families of other players on my dad's team or a few times with just my family, but this is very different. There's only about six people on this plane and suddenly I feel like this plane is entirely too small. As gorgeous as it is, I am freaking *nervous.*

I down the rest of my champagne in one gulp and when I set it down on the table in front of me, it's obvious my hand is shaking. "Hey," I hear from next to me, "Raegan, what's wrong, honey?"

I swallow, trying to keep the nerves from turning into tears and let out a deep breath. "I think I'm just a little nervous."

"Oh shit." I hear the hum of the plane and slowly feel us start to move. "Come here," he says. I get up on somewhat shaky legs and before I even take a step, his hand has wrapped around my wrist and pulled me across the aisle into his lap. "I'm sorry, I didn't even think about that."

"I'm not usually a nervous flier." My voice shakes slightly. "But usually, I'm with my family or friends or..." I let out a breath. "A much bigger plane with more people."

"We can fly commercial next time." He presses a gentle kiss on my lips and I instantly hate myself for how I'm coming off.

"No, I'm sorry." I press my hands to my forehead. "I didn't mean it like that. This is gorgeous and I am in awe of all of this."

"I get it. My parents refuse to get on my jet." He chuckles. "But I promise, it's safe and I hire the most competent and well-trained pilots." He grabs my hand and presses his lips to each finger one by one.

I nod as we start to taxi onto the runway. "Mr. Beckham, Miss Graham, I do hate to intrude—'' One of the flight attendants with glossy gorgeous dark brown hair and perfectly done make-up appears from the front of the plane where I assume they have their own space and Wes immediately looks at her from over his glasses.

"Then why are you?" His voice is laced with irritation and scolding and I feel bad for her even though I know she's about to make me move and I just got my heart rate to slow back down.

"We are about to take off and Miss Graham needs to take her seat."

"She's fine," he says, tightening his hold on me and pulling me against his chest to rest under his chin.

"She can return once we've—"

"*I said,* she's fine." I can't see his face from where I'm lying against him but I see hers which goes from irritation to acceptance in a matter of a second.

"Very well. We should be taking off in about ten minutes. Would either of you like anything?"

"Privacy for the next two hours and fifty minutes would be great," he says as he begins to stroke my back.

She nods before going back to the front and shutting the curtain that separates us.

"Wes." I move my head from his chest and glare at him.

"You were shaking like a leaf when you got in my lap, you want to go back over there?" He raises an eyebrow at me and I look at my chair across the aisle and then back to him before I reach for his glass of champagne and down it.

"Fine, but be nice."

He chuckles and lets me snuggle against him. I shut my eyes, trying to will us to Miami faster, and somehow, between those two glasses of champagne, and the warmth of Wes' arms around me as he strokes my back gently, I'm asleep before we take off.

I open my eyes and the first thing I see are clouds. The second thing I feel is Wes' hand still rubbing me gently. I do my best to tilt my head and when I look up, I see he's staring at his phone which is in the other hand. His eyes dart to me and a smile breaks out on his face as he puts his phone down on the tray in front of us. "Hey, sleepyhead. Feel better?" He cups my face and presses his lips to mine.

I nod, still slightly disoriented. "How long have I been out?"

He turns his wrist to look at his watch. "About an hour. That was impressive, I don't think I've ever seen someone fall asleep so fast. I was talking to you and then you were just out." He nods towards the food behind us. "Are you hungry?"

"No…" I shake my head and sit up. "You could have woken me or moved me if you had work to do."

He narrows his eyes like that was the most absurd thing he'd ever heard. "You were nervous and sitting in my lap seemed to help. I wish that could cure every problem you had."

The nerves have slowly faded away as it's really setting in just how bad this man has it for me. Part of me thinks it's just because it's new and exciting and I'm young, *far younger than him.*

But another part, the part that's a hopeless romantic just like my dad, thinks that this has the potential of turning into something real despite all the obstacles that stand in the way of us being together. It's barely been a week since we first slept together and he has clothes at his place for me to wear when I stay over. He calls me baby or honey more than he calls me Raegan. He fucks me constantly without a condom like there wasn't a chance I could get pregnant. *We really should relax with that.*

He is absolutely not like any man I've ever been with. "Do you want to go back there?" I point to the bedroom and give him a sexy smile. "I just mean…if you want?"

"Oh, I fucking want." He stands up with me still in his arms and walks us to the bedroom, shutting the door behind us and sets me on my feet. I look out the circular windows, seeing the sun and the white fluffy clouds pass by.

"I've never joined the mile-high club," I tell him as I turn around and tap my zipper behind me for him to help me. He's behind me in an instant, slowly lowering the zipper as he presses his lips to my neck.

"How lucky I am to be the one who gets to initiate you."

My dress falls to my feet and he picks it up, draping it over a chair in the corner. He turns around just as I'm unbuttoning my blouse and I watch as he begins to undress. It only takes a minute before we are both naked and on the bed, him on top of me and me lying on the softest cashmere blanket I've ever felt.

I actually feel like I'm in heaven.

He moves down my body, kissing practically every inch of skin before he gets to my pussy. "You have the prettiest pussy." He drags his tongue along the seam before he uses his fingers to open me up. "I used to lie awake at night thinking about how you'd melt against my tongue."

My eyes flutter closed at his words. "Oh God."

"I hope I can make you squirt again." He swirls his tongue around my opening, penetrating me a few times and wiggling his tongue inside of me.

"Wes, fuuuuuck."

"Oh absolutely, but first, I need you to come while I lick your pussy."

"Yes." I moan as he flicks my clit.

"That's my girl." He groans against me. "Come for me. Grind that sexy cunt against my mouth and give me what I want."

I put a hand over my face. "Jesus, Wes. The things that come out of your mouth." *Really his mouth in general. The things this man can do with his tongue should be illegal.*

He flicks his tongue against me again and I cry out just as he slides two fingers inside of me. "So, fucking sweet. God, I love your scent Raegan. I wish I could bottle it and keep it with me to smell when you're not around."

"Oh my God, Wes!" I sit up on my elbows to watch him. I grab his hair, dragging my fingers through his silky sandy brown strands, and pull gently, wanting him to look at me. When his eyes meet mine, I feel like all the air leaves my lungs with the intensity in them.

"You're so beautiful," he says between licks. I don't think I've ever felt so vulnerable while being intimate. It feels like Wes can see everything, every thought I have in my brain, feel every feeling coursing through me, and it's as if his emotions have a direct line to mine.

No, it's just great sex. There's no way you're already feeling—

My thoughts on my very complicated feelings for my boss turned lover come to a halt when that familiar tingle shoots through me like a delicious warning.

"I think I'm going to come."

"Oh yes." He slides two fingers inside of me and curls them

upwards and I pull his hair a little harder as I feel my orgasm crash over me.

My toes curl and my legs start to shake as I move my hips in tandem with his mouth. "Oh my God, *Daddy*, please fuck me."

I don't hear his response because my orgasm is going on and on and on but I feel his tongue gently tickling and flicking my clit. I want to pull away because I'm so overstimulated that it's almost painful but he has a grip on my thighs and now he's attached his mouth to my sex.

"Please," I beg. "I need your dick."

"You do, huh? Give Daddy another one first." He continues his assault and when I look down, his eyes are back on mine and then his hands are on my tits. Some of his fingers are wet from being inside of me so now one of my nipples is wet from my orgasm and there's something so sexy about it. Like when he spit in my mouth.

That was so hot.

"I want to taste myself again." It's amazing how much Wes has changed me in just a week. I feel empowered and bold enough to ask for what I want which is something I've never felt. He makes me feel like this sex goddess that should have every single thing she wants.

He grins, just before he flattens his tongue and drags it slowly through my slit. "After you come," he tells me. "And then I'm going to put my dick here," he says as he rubs the top of my mound.

"Yes! I cry. "I want your dick inside me, Daddy." His licks get more aggressive and I think he's grinding his dick into the bed. "Oh fuck, I'm coming again. Yes yes yes." I cry out as he licks me through a second orgasm. My clit is still pulsing even after he pulls away from my sex and moves up my body. He squeezes my jaw, forcing my mouth open again and he lets my cum drip lazily into my mouth from his. He spits a bit more into my mouth before he drags his tongue along my bottom lip.

"You can't tell anyone I touched you like this, Princess. They'll take you from Daddy." He bites down on my bottom lip and I groan at how dirty and sexy this is and also kind of a parallel to what's actually going on between us. While no one could take me from Wes, they could certainly fire me, and who knows what they could do to him even though he owns the company.

"I won't tell anyone, Daddy. Our secret," I whisper just before his lips land on mine.

"Can I put my dick inside you, baby?"

"Yes, please," I beg, already anticipating the roaring orgasm I'm going to have.

He moves off of me and before I can protest, he's flipped me over and brought me up to my knees before landing a slap on my ass. My mouth falls open and a gasp tumbles out just as I clench my pussy at the sexiness of it. He spanks me a little lower. "Is this okay?"

"Yes," I manage to sputter out as lust takes over.

"Tell me if it's too much." I nod and he spanks me again. "Words."

"Yes, Daddy!"

"Good girl. Do you think you can come for me like this?" He asks as he moves his hand a little lower and manages to land a smack on my sex. "Put your ass up higher." I do as he tells me, forcing my face into the pillows and I feel another smack on my sex, so close to my clit. I shift, pushing my ass up higher and I hear a chuckle and then his lips on my ass cheek followed by his tongue. "Have you ever had anything in your ass, honey?"

"No," I whimper.

"Well, don't worry, I won't put anything there tonight, but is that something you'd want to do?"

"Like…your dick?" I ask, and I hear the slight apprehension in my voice.

"We'd work up to that. We'd start with my tongue and my fingers." He squeezes my ass cheeks.

"There?" I squeak and while I know that's a thing people do, I hadn't ever expected I'd ever be one of them. I mean I'd showered this morning but it's so…dirty. I swallow nervously at the thought of his tongue in my asshole. *Fuck that sounds hot.*

"Yes, Angel. Daddy wants to touch you and lick you here but only if you're okay with it."

I let out a shaky breath. "Can we talk about this when I'm not so horny I can barely think?"

I feel his dick at the entrance to my cunt as he drags it through my seam. "Yes, baby, of course."

He pushes inside of me with a force that moves me up the bed. "Oh my G—God." I stammer. I've always loved sex from behind and with how big his dick is, it allows him to get so deep that I'm ready to come after only a few thrusts. "I'm already there."

"Fuck, I know you are. You're squeezing me so tight."

My eyes slam shut as my third orgasm is already dancing underneath my skin and fireworks are going off behind my eyelids. "Daddy, please."

"Please what, baby?"

"Come inside me."

"Fuuuuck. Baby, don't tempt me."

"I want it. *Please.*" I hear myself beg and I feel like I'm having an out of body experience because *what the fuck am I saying?*

"You're just caught up in the sex high." He fucks me harder with each thrust, his fingers digging into my hips. "We can talk about that too after you come."

I let out a whine. "But—"

"I want nothing more than to fill you up right now. Come

inside this pretty cunt that I've been obsessed with since long before I even touched it. But not yet." He pulls me harder against him and I bite my bottom lip.

"Yet?"

"You know I will. I'll come so much it'll drip out of you and then I'll push it back in because it all belongs inside."

"Oh fuck!" My arms shake as my orgasm pulls me under. I cry out again when he goes even deeper and taps the spot that makes my eyes roll back and my clit splinters under the friction. "Oh my God, fuck I'm coming." I'm pushing back against him just as hard and I hear him groan when I clench and spasm around him.

I reach between my legs to fondle his balls, and he lets out a guttural groan. "Ohhhh fuck me, Raegan." His voice is hoarse and sexy and makes my clit react like it's trained to know what that voice means. "Your pussy is going to make Daddy come. You're such a good fucking girl." *This is so fucking hot.* "I have to pull out though."

I nod because I'm starting to come down from the high of my climax and obviously, yes, he needs to pull out.

"Jesus, baby, you're incredible." He groans as his thrusts get more erratic and then he pulls out and I feel a rush of warmth on my back. I feel him breathing behind me and I stay still so I don't spill his cum that's all over me. "Wow." He breathes and then he's off the bed and I hear water running. He returns in an instant, wiping my back with a warm washcloth and then he's on the bed, pulling me against him.

"That was amazing."

He strokes my back and I look up into his gorgeous eyes. "I agree." He props his head up on a fist and stares down at me. "I almost came inside of you."

"Sorry about that." I blanche remembering what I said when I was moments from climaxing.

"It was hot." He reaches down and sucks one of my breasts into his mouth before letting it go with a pop. "One day, I'll come inside of you, lick both of our orgasms out of you, and then spit it into your mouth." He gets up like he'd just said the most normal thing in the world and not the most salacious thing I've ever heard.

Well, minus the whole ass eating thing.

He moves towards the shower and I gasp. "Wes!" He shoots me a smirk as he opens the shower door and turns on the water. I stare at him as the water hits his hard body and drips down his cock. I understand the reasoning now behind the see-through glass because I almost want to watch him more than I want to join him. He turns to face me like he heard my thoughts.

"You going to watch or join me?" He asks.

"I'm not sure yet." But I doubt he can hear me over the water so I just shrug. I stare at his dick, my eyes zoning in on his piercings before letting them move all over him. He shoots me that sexy grin with those goddamn dimples that should be illegal before turning back around to give me a view of that delicious ass that I suddenly wanted to bite.

Dear God, he is gorgeous and so freaking sweet and considerate. I melt thinking about him holding me during takeoff. I mentally add that to the very long list of things that make him so perfect. *How isn't he married?*

I'm off the bed to open the door, but I don't enter the shower. I just stand in the entryway.

"There she is." He moves towards me and holds out his hand but I don't take it.

"Why aren't you married?"

Chapter TEN

WES

WELL, I WASN'T EXPECTING THAT.

I mean I was expecting this conversation at some point but not right after sex. Certainly not right after *that* kind of sex.

"You want to talk about this now?"

"You're just so…perfect." She crosses her arms over those delicious tits and my eyes drop to them, lazily dragging my eyes over the creamy skin. "How has no woman realized that?"

I pull my eyes away from them and switch off the water, my dick already retreating because it knows it won't be spending time inside Raegan anytime soon. I grab the towel on the hook and wrap it around my waist as I stand in front of her. "I'm not perfect."

She purses her lips before she sits on the bed and wraps the blanket around her. "You know what I mean."

I sit next to her and grab her hand, pulling it to my lips. "I've never been like this with another woman before." I sigh because I'm not sure what else to say. I don't want to say that she's different because I don't know how to explain why that is. "I've never cared about whether a woman thought I was perfect."

She shakes her head and puts her hands on my chest. "You don't have to try to be perfect by the way." She sits back on her heels and chuckles. "Even though you are."

I smile and press my lips to hers. "I'm certainly not." I tell her before I stand to dry off and get dressed.

"What flaw do you have? Besides leaving the thermostat on sixty-five in December—but we can work on that."

I shoot her a look. "Oh, we can?"

"Don't you want me to stay over?" She sasses.

"Don't *you* want my tongue in your cunt?" I shoot back without even looking at her as I grab some briefs from my suitcase, and she scoffs.

"Rude!" She's silent before she speaks up again. "How many serious relationships have you had?"

"How many have you had?" I ask her.

"Two," she responds. "But I'm twenty-one."

"Yes, twenty-two next month," I say, remembering her feisty comment from the holiday party.

"Don't be cute." She gets up and starts to get dressed as well.

"I've had a few more."

"I would assume that with having a few years on me."

"I was engaged once," I tell her. I want to be completely transparent about Hannah so I guess it's time to get it all out in the open. I have nothing to hide and I certainly wouldn't want to hide anything from Raegan.

"Did you end it?" She asks as she slides a new thong up her legs.

"No, we're still together," I joke as I begin to button my shirt.

She glares at me and I laugh as she swats my hand away and begins to button them for me. "You know what I mean."

"I initiated it technically, but she was on board. We both decided it was time. The last year we were together was really hard. We fought all the time and I was the most unhappy I'd ever been." I sigh as I think about that time in my life. "I was stressed about work and I was just so miserable, but we ended it, and I saw a therapist for a while, and everything seemed to settle after that."

"You have a therapist?"

"I do. I don't see her often, but I think it's important. I was angry at my parents for a while for some things and I wanted to let that go. I was very overwhelmed and overworked when I was getting my company off the ground, so she was good for that as well." I shrug. "And then again when everything happened with Hannah."

"Wow. That is really mature. I feel like some men won't freely admit that." I pull on my slacks and watch as she pulls a bra on over her tits. "So, just the one relationship?" She raises an eyebrow like she's not buying that.

"That's my most recent and my most serious, but I dated a few women years ago in college and after that." She nods. "What happened with yours?"

"Well, I dated a guy for three years in high school and my freshman year of college and you know how that goes." She rolls her eyes. "We went to different colleges and..." She trails off.

"You drifted apart?"

She shoots me a look. "If by that, you mean he *drifted* into another girl's vagina, then sure."

I was hoping that wasn't where she was going with that although I had a sneaking suspicion it was. "Sounds like a dick."

"Oh, he was." She chuckles. "My college boyfriend was only marginally better." She slides on her dress and turns around so I can zip her up and I'm already trying to figure out when I can zip it down.

"I'm sorry." I press a kiss to her neck.

A voice breaks through the tension and I realize it's the flight attendant through the loudspeaker. "Good morning, Mr. Beckham, Miss Graham. We are preparing for our landing. If you are able, we would love if you would take your seats. If you are unable, we advise that you not use any of the bathroom features, and to stay seated, thank you!"

Raegan giggles and grabs my hand. "This was the most fun I've ever had on a plane. Thank you. I would be willing to fly on this again, so long as we can make use of the bedroom."

"Believe me, Raegan, when you and I are on a plane, we will be making very good use of any bed on board."

An hour later, we are walking towards the concierge desk of the Four Seasons Hotel in Miami with her hand encased in mine. After tomorrow, I won't be able to touch her freely for three days so I'm relishing in doing so now. We make it to the front desk and a woman gives us a bright smile.

"Mr. Beckham, welcome back. I'm April. Thank you for choosing us again for your stay. As a valued member of the Four Seasons family, it's always lovely to see you. How was your travel from Philadelphia?"

"Great." I give her a polite smile and pull Raegan closer to me.

"Lovely to hear. The presidential suite is all ready and the rest of the rooms will be ready tomorrow upon your team's arrival." She looks at her computer. "They are expected around noon?"

I nod. "Yes, that's correct. Mr. Holt should be checking in sometime this evening."

"Excellent, his room is also ready." She lifts a tray with two champagne flutes and sets it on the counter. "Here are your keys, and your luggage is being delivered to your room as we speak. Is there anything else I can assist you with at this time?"

"No, that's all, thank you." I grab them both and hand one to Raegan which she takes as I begin to usher her towards the elevator when she stops.

"Wait," she looks at me and then April, confused. "I should have a room as well. Is mine ready yet?"

April frowns. "I'm sorry, I thought only Mr. Beckham's room was needed at this time." She begins typing into her computer and I realize now I probably should have told Raegan what I did.

"Pardon me for just a second," April says, probably starting to panic that she can't find a record for a reservation for her room.

"It's not necessary," I tell her. "We only need one room."

"But I booked—" Raegan starts.

"I canceled it," I tell her before turning back to April. "We are all set, thank you very much."

"Oh, wonderful," April says with an obvious sigh of relief. "Please call us if you need anything. We have made a note that you will need a car around seven-thirty tonight?"

"Correct."

"Wonderful, enjoy your stay," she says with a nod as I lead Raegan away from the desk.

"You canceled it?" She asks as we walk through the massive lobby.

"Yes, did you think you were staying in a different room tonight?"

"Well, no." She bites on her bottom lip. "But I need to stay in my own room tomorrow."

"Do you?" I ask her as I press the button for the elevator.

"Yes, what if someone wants to come to my room?"

"Who would want to come to your room?" I ask, my mind immediately going to that tool Liam wanting to come upstairs with her.

"Marissa?"

"Go to hers." I shrug.

"Wes!"

I roll my eyes. "I didn't cancel your room for tomorrow, relax. Though, the fact that you want to sleep away from me is not sitting well with me." I guide her into the elevator with my hand on her lower back and scan my key against the censor to access the private floor.

"Wes, that's not it."

I press her against the wall. "Then, what is it?"

"I don't want to get caught leaving your room?" She looks up at me. "I would love to stay in your room with you the whole time we are here, but you know it's not that simple."

"You wouldn't get caught. Only my room and Chris' room are on this floor and it requires a key for access." I hold up the black metal key card for her to see.

"It's not just that."

"I know, which is why you still have your own room. That I'll have a key to." I lean down and press a kiss to her lips just as the elevator dings and the door opens.

"Think you're going to sneak into my room?"

"If you're not willing to sneak into mine, yes. I'm not going three days without touching you when you're two floors away, Raegan Graham."

"Oh, my full name?" She giggles as we move towards my suite that takes up a good fourth of the floor.

"This is for you." I hand her a key. "In case you do want to sneak up here." I wink at her and she bites her bottom lip before slipping it into her purse.

We enter the suite which is the usual one I stay in when I'm here. It consists of a master bedroom, a master bathroom as well as a guest bathroom, a dining and living area, and a small kitchen. Our luggage is already inside and there's another bottle of champagne as well as the chocolate-covered strawberries and a cheese plate that I ordered.

"I feel like you're trying to get me drunk," Raegan says as she puts the glass we'd gotten downstairs on the table. "I was going to take a shower. I know you took one on the plane, but do you want to watch?"

"Oh fuck." I chuckle. "I would love that, but I have a call in about fifteen minutes." I sigh.

"Oh! Do you need me?"

"No." I shake my head. "Take a shower, relax, take a nap if you want. I really don't think I'll need you until everyone else is here. I just like to get here a day early, mostly to prepare for tomorrow."

"I see. Well, if you need me for something let me know?"

"I will definitely need you for something." I smack her butt and she giggles before she rolls her suitcase towards the bedroom.

About an hour later, Raegan comes out of the bedroom, dressed in a black high-waisted mid-length skirt and a white blousy t-shirt tucked in and she looks so effortlessly gorgeous. Her hair is pulled up into a ponytail and despite the person talking in my ear, I find myself transfixed by her moving around the living room. I'm seated at the desk in the living area, just watching her when her eyes meet mine. She gives me a sweet smile before moving towards me.

I move back from the desk and look down at my lap

indicating I want her to sit and she points at the phone. "I'm on mute."

"Shouldn't you be listening?" She asks just as I pull her onto my lap and she wraps her arms around my neck.

Her scent overwhelms me in the best way. It's sexy and makes me want to find the nearest surface to fuck her on. "You smell good."

She kisses my nose and then my mouth. "So do you."

She goes to move off of my lap when I hold her in place and turn my phone off mute. "I need to take a call, I'll be back on in ten minutes," I say before hanging up the phone without waiting for their reply.

"Is there really another call?" she asks and I glare at her for already knowing me well.

"I need to talk to you about something and that takes precedence. They were just talking bullshit. They're lucky I had something else that required my attention more at the moment." I reach into my pocket and pull out my wallet. "I need you to do something for me."

"Of course, anything. That's why I'm here." She tries to move again, probably trying to find that line between my assistant and the woman I'm sleeping with but I hold her steady.

"So, you see I already got my assistant something for Christmas, but in the last week our relationship has..." I rub my lip, trying to find the best word, "*changed*. So, I don't think the gift I got her is really appropriate." I open my wallet and pull out a black American Express card. "Do you think you can go pick something out for her? Spare no expense, I'm *crazy* about her."

She looks at the card and then back to me, realizing what I want her to do. "Wes..."

"Miss Graham," I respond, using the voice I haven't used on her since the first time I kissed her.

"Wes, you don't have to—"

"Mr. Beckham."

She glares at me. "Oh, it's Mr. Beckham, now? You do realize I'm still seated in your lap?"

I pull my glasses off and slide them on the desk in front of us. "Miss Graham, this is your job. Are you telling me you can't do this?" I ask her.

She shakes her head. "I'm telling you that you don't have to do this."

I know that. "But I want to and I *can.* Let me spoil you."

She looks at the credit card and pulls it gently from my fingers then turns her gaze back to me. "I don't want you to think this is necessary to keep me…interested."

I nod. "Yes, I know. I'm aware my dick does that plenty."

She runs her hands through my hair and presses a kiss to my lips. "It's not just your dick."

I smile. "My sparkling personality does it, huh?"

She scrunches her nose. "I was going to say the dimples. The personality is a hit or miss." She gives me a cheeky smile and I glare at her before lifting her off my lap and landing a slap on her ass. "Fine, I'll go. Can you give me a budget?" She spins the card around her fingers and I lean back in my chair, wanting to tell her no, but knowing that won't go over well.

Fuck it. Let's see. "I don't want to give you a number. Buy whatever you want."

She puts her hands on her hips and my dick jumps in response like it wants its own chance to convince her. "A number or I'm not going."

I slide my glasses back on my face already irritated that I have to get back on this call and I can't go with her. "Fine. Five hundred thousand. But if you want to go over—"

"Oh my God, I will absolutely not go over that," she shrieks.

"Try," I command as I open up my laptop.

She lets out a sigh of defeat and holds the card up between her fingers staring at it before shooting me a devilish look. "Five hundred thousand, huh? Can we go shopping in Paris?"

Now there's an idea. Thoughts of making love to her in my favorite city in the world and hearing her speak French makes my dick thicken in my slacks and my heart race.

Wait, did I just say make love?

"Name the day." I pull up my calendar and look for a window when I could take a few days to go to Paris. "As a matter of fact, do you want to leave straight from here? We'll have a few days and I can have you back home in time for Christmas," I tell her. "Say the word."

Her mouth drops open and she blinks her eyes at me. "You are insane."

I'm out of my chair, crossing the room and then I have her in my arms. "You said you want to go, and I want to take you. I can finally hear you put that French minor to use."

She gasps. "You remembered that?"

I lift her off her feet so that we're at eye level. "I thought I made it pretty clear that I have been very aware of you since you started. I remember everything in regards to you."

It's about three-thirty when I finally finish all the work I'm doing for the day. I pull up my credit card app just to make sure she's actually shopping and I'm impressed to see that she's actually buying some things. I've seen the way she dresses; I know Raegan has expensive taste and I'm happy to indulge her.

Me: Hey gorgeous

Raegan: Hi!

Me: Are you having fun?

Raegan: You let me loose in Miami with a credit card, of course I am.

Me: And I had to practically beg you to do it.

Raegan: I bought something better to wear for tonight, want to see?

Me: Of course. Show me.

I'm taking a sip of the water in front of me when a picture of her in the skimpiest piece of white lacy lingerie I've ever seen crosses my screen causing me to almost choke on the liquid. The brassiere part is almost completely sheer except on the straps and the cups beneath her breasts allow me to make out her pink nipples through the material. The bottoms are the same, except there's a satin bow at the top of her mound preventing me from really seeing too much of her cunt. There's a second picture that's of her back which is basically just her ass with what I can only surmise to be dental floss between her cheeks. There's another bow at her lower back and my dick is suddenly painfully hard.

I'm pressing her contact without another thought. "Hello?" she says and I can hear the innocence in her voice, like she's trying to act like she has no idea why I'm calling her.

"Don't hello me." I grab my wallet and am out the door towards the elevator. "Where are you?"

"*Cartier*." She giggles. *She expects me to believe she took that picture at a jewelry store?*

"That is absolutely not a *Cartier*," I say as I begin to pace the elevator, willing it to go down faster.

"Well, I took that picture an hour ago."

The elevator dings and I'm out of it almost running through the lobby. "Did you get the lingerie?"

"I did."

"You said you got something to wear for tonight, I thought you meant something for our date."

"Oh…I was planning to wear that to dinner. No good?"

I chuckle as I move towards the valet. "Can you call me a car? I'm in the Presidential suite."

"Of course, sir." A kid—probably no older than twenty—says as I notice he points towards a black car that's parked.

I hear a giggle through a phone. "Are you coming here?"

"You sent me a picture of you in lingerie. You basically demanded me to come." The black car pulls up and I slide into the back. "What are you getting at *Cartier*?" I lower the phone to speak to the driver. "Going to the Design District, please. Thanks."

"Nothing, I was just looking. My dad usually buys my jewelry."

Not for much longer, Miss Graham.

"I should be there in about ten minutes."

"Okay, I'm going to *Valentino* to look at shoes."

When I get to the store, I see a car out front with a man a little older than I am, standing in front of the passenger side door and I have a sneaking suspicion that's who's been driving Raegan around.

"Mr. Beckham." He nods.

"You've been with Miss Graham?"

He smiles. "Yes, sir. Lovely young lady. Reminds me of my daughter."

"She's amazing." I look towards the door and then back at him. "Thank you for driving her."

"Of course." He nods and then I'm moving towards the store. The guard opens the door and then I'm inside where I'm greeted with an overzealous associate and a practically empty store.

"Welcome to *Valentino,* how can I help you today?"

My eyes scan the store looking for her but I don't see her. "I'm looking for someone." The urge to say *girlfriend* hits me hard but I refrain.

"Oh! Raegan?"

"Yes." I nod at her.

"Follow me. She's in the dressing room."

Fuck. I follow behind her to the back of the store and the thought of her behind one of these red velvet curtains getting undressed has my dick thickening with anticipation each step I get closer to her. "Raegan, you have a visitor!"

She peeks her head out of a curtain and gives me a smile. I don't see anything except her feet in nude heels and a bit of her legs. The associate has disappeared giving the illusion that we are alone even though I wonder if there are people in other dressing rooms.

"Want to come in?"

I don't even respond, I just push past the curtain, shutting it behind us. I almost drop to my knees when I see she's completely naked save for those very sexy heels. "Fuck," I whisper, my eyes moving all over her body like I've never seen her nude before. She has on a bit more makeup than when she left, making me wonder if she went somewhere to get it done. Her lashes look ten times longer than usual, her lips are painted red, and I'm already picturing my dick the same color.

"Do you like the shoes?" she asks, looking down at her feet.

My eyes drop back to her feet, completely forgetting what they even looked like.

"Yeah," I croak as I take a step towards her but she doesn't move backwards.

"I'm glad you're here."

"You are?"

"Mmmmhm, you can help me pick out which shoes."

"Get them all." I wrap my arms around her and burrow my nose in her hair. I kiss her soft pouty lips and I don't waste another second before I drop my hand between her legs and swipe my index finger through her slit.

Her eyes dart up to meet mine and I press my index finger to her lips. Her tongue darts out and drags up my finger, licking the tip in that sexy way she does to the tip of my cock.

A devilish smile finds my face and I shake my head at her, deciding if she's going to play dirty then I'm going in for the kill. I push her against the mirror in the dressing room and drop to my knees before she can protest, pressing my mouth to her cunt. She lets out a shaky breath. "Wes," she whispers, and it sounds something like scolding mixed with a plea.

I go back to fucking her with my tongue when the associate returns. "Everything okay?"

I look up and see Raegan's eyes shut, her cheeks pink, and her bottom lip between her teeth. Her eyes flutter open. "What?" she asks.

"She's going to get the shoes." I look around the room and see that she's got three boxes in here and two dresses. I drag my tongue through her slit. "All the shoes…" I flick her clit and stare up at Raegan who nods her head. "And the dresses?" She shakes her head no. "Never mind, not the dresses."

"Great! Did you want to see anything else?" She asks.

I blow gently on Raegan's sex and she puts a hand over her mouth. "No, I don't think so. We'll be out in a second."

I hear her heels walking away.

"Oh, Wes," she whispers, and I stand up, putting my fingers back inside of her. I hold one arm out against the wall, while the other is between her legs.

"So fucking perfect." I press my lips to her neck and her nipples brush against my torso and I wish more than anything I didn't have this polo shirt on so I could feel her sweet tits on my skin.

"I think I'm going to come, baby." She moans as she lets her head fall back against the mirror. My eyes widen as my brain takes notice that it's the first time she's called me something besides my name or *Daddy.*

Fuck me.

"Raegan, baby, look at me. Let me see those blue eyes when you go over."

She lets out a quiet moan and her eyes flutter open just as she wraps a leg around me opening her up. "Will you fuck me when we get back to the room?" She asks, her voice soft and breathy and it messes with the restraint that's preventing me from taking my dick out and fucking her right here in this dressing room.

"The second we're through the door."

"And tomorrow?"

"Whenever you want." I drop a kiss on her lips, careful not to ruin her lipstick even though I wish I could slide my tongue through her lips and smear it everywhere. "You tell me when."

She wraps her arms around me and pushes her face into my neck. "All I have to say is jump, huh?" she jokes, letting her tongue dart out to lick my jaw.

"How high?" I grunt as I stroke my thumb over her clit and she gasps.

"Oh God." She moans and then she shudders. I take my hand

off the wall and wrap it around her as she shakes in my arms. "Wes, right there!" she whines.

She finally stops convulsing and I pull my fingers from her and push them into my mouth. We share a smile before she begins picking up her clothes. I help her into them and pick up the shoes to carry them to the counter. She hands me my card as we leave the dressing room. "Thank you by the way."

"For the orgasm?" I ask her and she rolls her eyes.

"No, if anything, you should be thanking *me* for that," she says with a sexy smirk.

"You want me to thank *you* for giving you an orgasm?"

"Yes, because I think you enjoy mine more than I do," she jokes and I swat her ass even though she's not far off from the truth on how much I enjoy making her come. I put the shoe boxes on the counter and hand the associate my card. "I meant thank you for the shoes," she tells me and nods towards the door, "and everything else."

I cup her face and press my lips to hers. "Of course," I whisper against her lips, and when I turn back to the associate, she's looking at us with the dreamiest look.

"You guys are just so cute." She beams. "How long have you been together?"

Raegan's eyes flit away from her to me, probably wondering what I want to say. I rub my thumb just under her lip to where I actually did smear her lipstick a little. "A while," I say, with my eyes still trained on Raegan.

Which in my eyes is not a lie.

Chapter ELEVEN

Raegan

IT'S NEARING SEVEN AND I'M ALMOST FINISHED GETTING ready. I had to banish Wes to the other bathroom because I wasn't getting anything done with the way he was pawing at me. I didn't like getting dressed until last, and he was proving that he couldn't be around me while I was doing my hair and makeup. I was just in my bra and underwear because I'd forgotten the silky robe I usually wear and he'd tried to take my panties off twice *while I was holding my curling wand!*

It's a wonder I didn't burn either of us.

I'm finally done with my hair and touching up my makeup, after putting a little bit more time into everything tonight and pull out the dress I found while I was out earlier. It's sexier and shorter than what I usually wear but Miami is another world and I would probably still be the most covered person out tonight. It's a lime green satin dress with a completely open back that comes to mid-thigh. It shows a hint of cleavage, but I'm mostly covered there since *everywhere else* is exposed. The shoes I had matched perfectly, are open-toed and tied around my ankle.

I look at myself in the mirror and am a little shocked at the woman looking back at me. *Holy fuck.*

I know that I have a nice body but I rarely show this much of it. The most I've ever shown was during dance performances and that was only for four minutes a week.

I turn to look at myself in the mirror from all angles. "Wes!" I call for him and I smell his sexy cologne before he even walks into the room.

"You rang—" His voice cuts off and he stops in his tracks. I've never seen someone so obviously eye fuck someone but I might as well be naked with the way he's looking at me. "Holy fuck." He reaches for my hand and spins me around. "Oh my God. You're trying to kill me. Or you're trying to get someone killed because I will murder anyone that looks at you sideways."

A chuckle leaves my lips and I turn to look at him. "So, I look okay then?"

He pinches the bridge of his nose. "Okay? Raegan...I have three degrees and I don't even know what word explains how gorgeous you look." His hands find the side of my dress. "Are you wearing underwear?"

I nod. "Of course. Do you see how short this dress is?"

"Okay, thank fuck." He lets out a breath. "I need a drink." He walks away from me and I follow behind him.

"Wait, me too!"

I follow him to the bar area and watch him pour some whiskey in a glass. He downs it in one gulp. "Did they have that in other colors?"

I look down. "I think black...?"

"Go back and get it. Get it in every color. Get this color again too, because I might destroy this getting it off of you later." He traces the strap on my shoulder. "You're so beautiful, baby."

I shudder under his touch and his words. "Thank you. You look very handsome too by the way," I say looking him over. "Understatement actually." I rove my eyes over him. He's wearing black slacks and a black buttoned-down shirt but the sleeves are rolled to his forearms and his tattoo on display makes my knees weak. I'm used to seeing his tattoo out because he's naked or completely covered up because he's in a suit, but this in-between is different.

"I'm not used to seeing this when you have clothes on," I tell him as I touch his arm. "It's so fucking hot."

I trace my fingers over the colorful tattoos interwoven all over his arm. When I look up, he's looking down at me with a look that tells me we might be late for the opening. "I don't think we have time and it took me a minute to get my hair to do what I wanted it to. I'm used to humidity but this shit down here is ridiculous." I have a hair tie and mini hairspray in my purse in case my hair doesn't survive but I would like for it to look nice at least through the lobby of the hotel.

He wraps his arms around me and presses his lips to mine. "Fine, and thank you."

"Can you pour me some whiskey?" I ask and he raises an eyebrow at me.

"You don't like whiskey."

"I didn't say that, I said I'm not a whiskey drinker and I just think it might take the edge off some."

"The edge?"

"My nerves. The fact that I'm horny and you look like that." I wave my index finger up and down his body.

He chuckles. "Yeah, I'm the problem."

"I'll bet you're hit on just as much as I am." I run my hands up his chest and he grabs them pulling me closer to him.

"No one is going to hit on me with you right next to me, and if some guy hits on you I'm going to jail."

"Wes." I shake my head.

"I'm not kidding." He pours me a smaller glass of whiskey and hands it to me. "Sip—" he starts just as I tip it back like a shot. "Okay then." He nods, with a playful look in his eye.

"What?" I shiver, squeezing my eyes shut as it goes down and I let out a little cough. "Do we have anything I can use for a chaser?"

He laughs and shakes his head. "Baby, you don't chase Macallan eighteen."

"Wesley." I deadpan.

His eyes widen and he puts a hand over his heart. "My full name?" He reaches under the bar and pulls out a ginger ale and a coke and I grab the ginger ale, before pulling it to my lips to take a sip, swishing the taste out of my mouth.

"God, you're fucking cute. You want another one?"

"I'm good." I scrunch my nose. "We should go or we're going to be late."

He clasps our hands together, bringing my hand to his lips as we start walking towards the door. "Thank you for coming with me."

I stop in my tracks. "Oh wait, did I have a choice?" I give him an innocent smile.

He rolls his eyes and pulls me through the door. "Nope, come on."

Miami at seven-thirty is notorious for horrible traffic, so we are sitting in it in the back of a town car when Wes' phone rings.

"Oh, this fucker." He groans and I assume it's Chris. "Yes?" He's silent for a moment, "No." His hand, which is wrapped around my thigh tightens. "Because I said so. You'll be fine. I have plans." I giggle, assuming Chris is trying to tag along with us wherever we are going and Wes is having none of it. "If you want to come to the gallery opening, fine, but you're not coming to dinner." I trace my fingertips over his knuckles and he squeezes my thigh. "No, we don't want to go out. Sure. Okay, call me when you're outside," he says before hanging up.

"You're so grumpy even with your best friend?"

"He annoys me more than anyone." He chuckles. "Though, he's just pressing me about tonight because he wants to be nosy about you."

"I figured as much. You told him about us?"

"I told him six months ago when I hired you." That shocks me. I didn't know men usually talked about their crushes like that. "Then at the holiday party, I couldn't stop staring at you. That's why he came to get me when I was talking to you and Marissa. He said I was staring at you like I wanted to fuck you."

"I remember when he came to get you. I didn't realize that was about me." I feel my cheeks heat thinking about that night and my heart flutters remembering him telling me that he couldn't stop thinking about me.

"Then we disappeared around the same time and I avoided his calls for two days so he put two and two together."

"I can't believe that was less than a week ago." *Because as close as it feels we've gotten, you would think it's been months.* "But you could have invited him to dinner."

"No, I would not like my pain in the ass best friend there for our first date."

"Well, we have already slept together, so we could delay our first date if you wanted."

"I do not want, and Chris knows a million and five people here. He'll be fine." He shakes his head as we finally break through the traffic.

A short while later, we are walking through the gallery, him with a whiskey and me with a glass of champagne. "So, are you going to buy anything?"

"If something looks nice, I guess. I don't know much about art to be honest, but I guess I should, since they're a big client." He shrugs and looks around the room. It's almost exactly what I expected. It's like a museum with art all over the walls and sculptures in each room. The walls are a deep charcoal gray, giving the room a darker feel and there are lights hanging from the ceiling, giving it an industrial look. "You see something you like?"

"Me?"

"Sure, if it's something that's going to be at my house, you're going to have to look at it too."

I wonder if I'm visibly swooning right now.

"I'll let you know if something speaks to me."

"Wes Beckham!" I hear a high-pitched voice from behind us and when I turn around, I see a woman with long red hair in a white strapless cropped top that looks more like a bra and leather leggings that look like they are painted on her coming towards us. "Darling!" She presses a kiss to each of his cheeks. "I am so happy you could make it." Her sparkling green eyes flit to me. "Hello!" She kisses my cheeks as well. "I did hear you were bringing someone." She smiles at me and then at Wes. "Don't you two make a cute couple!"

"I—I'm his assistant." I blurt out although I wish I hadn't. There isn't anyone from work here and what were the chances we'd be back here with the team tomorrow? *Well, we might be?*

"Oh! Well, never mind!" She giggles and I can hear a faint Italian accent in her voice. "Thank you so much for coming."

"Lily Ricci, this is Raegan Graham," he looks at me, letting his eyes linger on me a beat longer, "my assistant." He blinks at me, giving me a look that says *that is not what you are.*

"Lovely to meet you. Your dress is gorgeous," she says turning back to Wes before I even have a chance to respond. "So, my manager thinks I need something for the back door? Maybe another camera? Can you come see?" She turns to me, "We'll be right back."

"No, she stays with me," Wes says immediately.

"Oh. Okay." She shrugs.

"I can wait here if that's easier?" I say and he glares at me before guiding me gently in front of him as we follow Lily through the gallery. Before we are even off the gallery floor, someone calls her name and she squeals before taking off in their direction. I stop walking not knowing where to go and Wes chuckles behind me.

"Typical," I hear him say. I turn around and he waves a hand. He looks me over and narrows his eyes over the glass of whiskey. "What's with wanting me to go somewhere without you?" He tilts my chin up to look at him. "First of all, it's rude and I wouldn't do that to you when you don't know anyone here. Secondly, I am not letting you out of my sight while you're wearing this dress. Thirdly, I go somewhere alone with her and suddenly you're thinking she's back there giving me a strip tease, and when I get back, you're all pissed when absolutely nothing happened." He puts a hand up. "No thanks."

I scowl at him because there *may* be some truth to that. "Has she ever flirted with you?"

He sighs. "Yes."

"Have you slept with her?"

"No." I look in the direction that she flitted off in and he turns my chin to look at him. "My assistant?"

"Well, I am."

"Yes, but you didn't have to say it."

"You wanted me to let her think we were a couple? What if it got back to someone from work?"

"It wouldn't and if it did, I'd say she was mistaken. I wasn't saying confirm it, I just wasn't going to say anything."

"Oh..." I let out a breath and take a sip of the champagne, wishing like hell I had something stronger. "I guess I'll let you field the questions regarding us."

About an hour later we are preparing to leave, having not seen Lily again and Wes having bought a painting that was ungodly expensive for his home office. It was of a woman submerged in the ocean, staring out into the water as the sun began to rise. I wasn't sure that it was particularly profound but it looked pretty and the colors were gorgeous.

"Every time I look at it, I'll think she's you." The woman has dark hair but you can't see any of her face so I suppose it could be.

He wraps an arm around me and kisses my temple, and I don't know if it's the second glass of champagne mixed with the whiskey from earlier or the fact that the more time I spend with Wes, I find myself getting drunk on *him,* but I pucker my lips wanting him to kiss me. He smiles before he leans down and presses his lips to mine. When we pull apart our eyes stay locked on each other like kissing in public somehow changed something. I'm just about to say something when a voice cuts through the mounting sexual tension.

"Wes! I had no idea you'd be here!" He tenses against me and I can see the irritation on his face when he turns his gaze towards one of the most gorgeous women I've ever seen in my life. She reminds me of my mother except with darker hair and glasses resting against her high cheekbones. She is incredibly chic and sophisticated and completely decked out in *Chanel.*

She looks so classy and I look like I'm going to a club. Awesome.

She moves towards him. "Aren't you going to hug me?" She pushes herself between us, unlike Lily who may have tried to flirt but it had been more subtle. She presses a kiss to his cheek and I hate the mark she leaves behind from her lipstick. Like she's marking her territory.

Over my dead body.

I want to rub my finger over the skin while giving her a look that says to *back off* but I have no idea who this is, if she saw us kissing, or what to even do now.

"Hello, Claire," he says curtly without even a polite smile on his lips.

"Why didn't you call me? You usually let me know when you're coming to town so we can have dinner. Is Chris with you? I can call Isabella; you know they always hit it off." She giggles, still not having acknowledged my presence. *And she knows Chris and I'm guessing they double date or something while they're in town?*

Or maybe they have an orgy.

The intrusive thought floats through my brain and I down the rest of my glass.

"Claire, this is Raegan Graham. Baby, this is Claire Hunter." The "baby" stuns me momentarily but a warm feeling shoots through me that he's sending her a signal that they would absolutely not be going to dinner or whatever it is they do when *he's in town.*

"Lovely to meet you," I say with a smile I'm desperately hoping looks genuine.

She takes my hand, putting her other hand on top of ours, and gives it a squeeze. "Oh, isn't she cute! A little young for you Wes, but good for you!" She drops my hand before rubbing one up and down Wes' arm. "Certainly, more polished than your last plaything."

Anger flares through me because *what a witch!* I do my best not to react to her comment but Wes tenses next to me. "Raegan is absolutely not a plaything, and I can also assure you, I'm never looking for your approval or your opinion on anything I do, Claire." He pulls me away from her and out of the art gallery before she can reply. He doesn't say anything as we start walking towards the valet and after he nods towards the attendant, he looks down at me. "I'm sorry."

"For what? You didn't do anything."

He tucks a hair behind my ear and drags his hand down my shoulder. He lets his hand drop and I already want his hands back on me. "I didn't even think to check if she'd be here but I never thought she'd approach me like that."

"Have you slept with her?" *Do you really want to know?*

"Yes."

"More than once?" *So, we clearly want our feelings hurt?*

"Yes."

"Was she your girlfriend?"

"No, not at all."

The relief that washes over me is short-lived as memories of what Liam said come rushing back to me. While I know neither he nor Claire are reliable sources, I do want to bring it up before the curiosity of his past gets the better of me. I take a deep breath, hoping that this isn't going to cause an argument. "You'd said before that you never dated or...messed around with anyone that worked for *Beckham Securities* until me."

"That's correct."

"I heard...well...I suppose there's a rumor that that is not... exactly true?" I blink at him.

He narrows his eyes at me just as our car is brought around. "Where's this coming from?"

"Well, Claire's comment about your so-called playthings."

"I do not have playthings, Raegan. That was her being petty and jealous and I know you know that."

"You know what I'm saying."

"I don't think I do, so can you please be clearer?" His voice is even and soft, not accusatory or angry.

"I…" I look behind him where the driver has opened the door. "We should go."

He doesn't move or even look in the direction of the car. "He can wait. Tell me what's wrong."

"Nothing!" I shake my head because I'm not really even sure what is wrong. It's obvious that Claire was jealous and while the comment about my age stung, should it have? I mean I am much younger than Wes.

"Do you want to know what I think?"

"I don't know, do I?" I raise an eyebrow at him.

"I think you're feeling a little insecure because someone I've slept with before reminded you that I wasn't a virgin when I met you."

"I knew you weren't a—"

"Missing the point." He interrupts. "See why it's better not to refer to yourself as my assistant? Think how that could have gone if we'd gone with that narrative." He cups my cheeks. "A lot more work for me," he jokes and I sigh.

"You're right. I suppose I just felt a little insecure."

"That's fair. As far as the rumors at the office, that's just what they are, *rumors*. I've never touched anyone that worked for me."

I nod in understanding. While I do feel silly for bringing this up now, I feel better knowing a little bit more about the women that came before me and the context of his relationships with them. "Does it bother you that there's a big difference in our ages?"

"No. Does it bother you?"

I wrack my brain, searching for any wayward thought I may have had over the past week but nothing comes to mind. "No…I mean…you are very close to my dad's age but…no. Should it bother us?"

He shrugs. "I don't think so. If it makes you feel better, I don't think of you as a twenty-two year old." He wraps an arm around me and guides me towards the car. "Except for that time, you chased very nice whiskey with soda…" He laughs.

Chapter TWELVE

Raegan

WE ARE WHISKED INTO A PRIVATE AREA THE second we arrive at the restaurant. It has a table, a small L-shaped couch, and another table, almost like we have our own private room but outside. We are on the roof with the most gorgeous view of the city as well as the water. It's a little cooler now that it's getting darker, but nothing compared to the frigid temperatures of Philadelphia in December. Even still, I'm wearing next to nothing and it's inching below sixty-five degrees.

"Are you cold? We can move inside," Wes says as he slides his jacket off and onto my shoulders. "There are heated lamps up here also."

"No, this view is insane." I look out over the city staring at the blue and green hues that shine from below. "It's so beautiful."

"You're so beautiful." When I turn away from the view, he's staring down at me, and for the hundredth time, *just today,* I melt.

He guides me towards the couch, pulling me into his lap and wraps his arms around me. "Do you trust me?" He asks me and I look down at him, wondering where he's going with this.

"Yes."

"Completely?"

"Yes, but you're not going to try and convince me to let you fuck my ass or something here, right?" My eyes pan the area we're in, and while we are mostly secluded there are people around, and who knows when our servers would show up.

He laughs and tightens his hold, running his hand up my bare leg gently. "No, I wasn't. We have to work up to fucking your ass in public."

My eyes widen at his words because I don't think I'll ever get there. "Okay, so why do you ask?"

"Tell me where you heard that rumor."

"Wes…"

"You said you trust me."

"Yes, but I'm not about to have you pissed at whoever said something."

He narrows his eyes. "I already have an idea."

"You have to promise you won't be a dick to them."

He scoffs and pushes his glasses up on his nose. I squirm because I've recently realized that watching him fiddle with them turns me on. "When am I a dick to anyone?"

I cock an eyebrow at him. "You are not a dick to me, I'll give you that, but I also know you're going to be annoyed and you're not particularly fond of this person."

"I knew it was that fucker Liam."

"Then why did you ask!"

He scowls and moves me in his lap so I'm straddling him. "He fucking wants you and it irritates me and you know what? He's got a lot of nerve because he's fucked half the women in sales."

I gasp and then giggle, "Why, Wesley Beckham, are you engaging in office gossip?"

"No, but I hear things too."

I press my hands to his chest and let my lips hover over his. "I trust you. I'm sorry if what I said earlier made you feel like I didn't."

He leans forward and rubs his nose against mine. "I just don't want you getting all worked up over anything or *anyone.* I want *you,* Raegan. I've wanted you for months and now that I have a chance with you, I'm not going to fuck it up. Yes, I have a past but I'm an open book about it. I'll always be one hundred percent honest with you regarding all of it."

The dinner last night might have been one of the best meals I've ever had. Wes knew exactly how to order and did so for me in the way men do that's sexy and not chauvinistic. Coupled with the company made it one of the best dates of my life. We'd gone back to the room and he'd fucked me almost frantically like he was trying to get three days' worth of sex into one night even though I knew this wouldn't be the last time while we were here.

The jarring sound of my alarm breaks me from the most delicious dream of Wes and I on a beach drinking margaritas. I rub my forehead wishing I hadn't had another whiskey when we got back to the room last night because I have a slight headache. I reach blindly for my phone, turning it off before reaching for Wes, surprised that I don't feel his arms around me. I frown when I'm met with sheets and then I hear him talking and I realize he may be on a call. It's only eight-thirty so I grab one of the long fluffy robes and make my way into the living area where I hear him talking. I stop in my tracks when I see Chris sitting on the couch completely dressed down in sweats and a backwards hat, and I thank every god there is that I decided to put a robe on because I contemplated walking out here naked.

Both of their eyes flit to me and Chris raises an eyebrow at me before turning back to Wes. "Didn't realize you had a sleepover." He smirks as he looks me over.

"I will absolutely rip your eyes from your head." He growls at him before he moves towards me. "Hey, beautiful." He cups my face and presses his lips to mine gently. "How did you sleep?"

"Good. I'm sorry, I thought you were out here alone," I whisper. "Good thing I didn't come out here naked." I chuckle.

I start to move back towards my room when I hear Chris' voice. "Wait wait!"

"What Chris?" Wes asks, his tone bored and laced with annoyance.

We stop walking and he makes his way towards us. "I wanted to introduce myself." He smiles and I frown before laughing nervously.

"Well, ummm…I think we've met," I joke and he shakes his head.

"Sure, we've met professionally, but now you're the woman that's got my buddy more sprung than I've seen him in the twenty years I've known him." He holds out his hand. "Call me Chris." I shake his hand and he squeezes mine. "Maybe not at the office though."

"Noted." I giggle and I look up at Wes wondering if he's going to be pissed that Chris said all of that.

"Alright, I'll see you guys downstairs for the welcome meeting," Chris says as he makes his way out of the suite.

"I'm sorry about that, we had some things to talk about."

"Why are you apologizing? It's almost as if we're here for work or something," I joke as he follows me back into the bedroom.

"Because I wanted to wake you up with my mouth on your pussy."

"I can safely say my pussy is tired."

"Even for a kiss?" He raises his eyebrow at me and I shake my head.

"Yes, even for a kiss. Do you know how many orgasms you gave me last night?" I joke as I slide my robe off and move towards the bathroom.

"I lost count after five." He follows me into the bathroom and pulls his t-shirt off over his head. "And you're acting like you want more." He lets his eyes move over me hungrily.

"I need to shower!"

"Can I join you?"

"Can you behave?"

"In a shower with you? Unlikely."

"Wes…" I warn.

"Raegan…" he says. "I have to be around you all day and can't touch you. Just let me play with your pussy for a little bit."

I open the glass door and turn on the water to the shower. "What's in it for me?"

"Besides an orgasm?" He sighs as he slides his sweatpants off leaving him naked. He strokes his hand over his dick and squeezes the tip. "How about this in your mouth?"

"Deal."

I move into the shower, once the water has warmed up and he follows me in pulling me against his chest. "I am *dreading* today."

"It'll be fine."

"It'll be a fucking nightmare."

"Well, you're going to have to get used to it." I chuckle. "What do you think it's going to be like when we get back to Philadelphia?" He doesn't say anything and when I turn around and meet his gaze, his lips are pulled into a straight line. "What?"

"I was going to talk to human resources when we got back."

"WHAT?" I shriek as my eyes widen to the size of saucers, I'm sure. " HR?"

"Yes?"

"Wh–what?" My heart flips thinking about getting fired and everyone in the company knowing why.

"You don't want me to?" The hurt is evident on his face and I shake my head not wanting him to get the wrong idea.

"It's not that. I just…what if they say you have to fire me?" My lip trembles, "I really love this job."

"If I go to them, I won't let them fire you, but if we get caught, it'll be harder for me to talk us out of it."

I wince. "What if people hate me? Or think I'm just trying to sleep my way to the top? What if they say I'm a whore that—"

"Then, *they* will get fired." He cups my face. "I won't let anyone say anything to you."

"You can't be around all the time to protect me and you shouldn't have to!"

"So what, you're suggesting we wait?"

"It hasn't even been a week, Wes."

"And we wouldn't have to make an announcement to the entire company over it, but I'd like to at least clue HR in that we're together." He furrows his brows. "Unless we're not…"

"We are," I tell him because the last thing I want him to think is that I don't feel what he feels. "But it's much easier for you. You say that you won't let them fire me, but there's a good chance you may not have a vote in that. They'll try to make an example out of me. *This is why we have no fraternization policies in place,*" I say, in my best HR voice.

"They won't."

"You don't know that, Wes."

"And very worst case scenario, I would take care of you, you wouldn't have to worry about that."

I gasp and pull out of his arms to glare at him. "That might be the dumbest thing I've ever heard you say! I don't need you to take care of me, Wes."

He closes his eyes and lets out a sigh probably realizing how I took it. "I know, that's not what I—fuck, I'm sorry. I didn't mean it like that. I just meant—"

"I know what you meant." I glare at him as I begin washing my body and he sighs.

"Fine, we can wait."

"What if in a few months you're over this? You'll be glad you didn't say anything."

"And now, that's the dumbest thing I've heard *you* say." He takes the loofah from my hands. I try to take it back and he holds it up high over my head before spinning me around to wash my back. "I'm never going to be over this or over you."

"Wes..."

"Maybe you'll be the one that'll eventually be over it..."

I turn around and stare up at him. "If I didn't know any better, I'd say you think you and I are a done deal." He shrugs and my mouth drops open. "Wes!"

"Raegan!" he says with the same level of shock.

"I'm serious."

"So am I."

I blink up at him wondering how in the hell we got here and so fast. It wasn't even a week ago when I was talking to Marissa about how he'd never touch me, and now he's in a shower in the nicest hotel in Miami damn near confessing his love for me.

"I don't think I'll ever be over you either," I tell him.

He smiles in response and wraps his arms around me, letting his hands rest on my ass as he squeezes them. "Well, that's a relief, but maybe you're right. We'll give it some time. A month max, Raegan, and then I tell them."

I nod, because if we're here now, in a month he'll probably be thinking about putting a ring on my finger and a baby in my belly.

Wait.

"I have a question."

He squirts some shampoo into his hands and begins washing his hair. "I have an answer."

"Just for my knowledge, you know, since it seems you have made all these decisions already." I clear my throat. "Do you want kids?"

He cocks an eyebrow. "Hypothetically speaking?" I blink at him. "Or yours?" He adds and my cheeks heat at the thought of having his baby. *So does my pussy.* "Hypothetically, no. Yours, yes." I bite my bottom lip and he gives me a smile before he tips his head back to rinse the soap from his hair. "I haven't thought about kids in years and figured that ship sailed but ever since I started fucking you raw it's definitely been on my mind."

"We should probably start being more careful." He shrugs as if we're talking about something casual and not practically the most life-affirming thing in the world. "I always wanted a big family."

"I'll give you as many as you want."

"Okay, I know I said I needed a break, but never mind." I let out a breath and reach up to grab his face to pull his lips to mine.

"Oh my GOD," Marissa says as soon as she sees me walking towards the conference room for our first meeting dressed in a gray skirt and matching blazer practically buzzing with excitement. I'd already switched to the room I *should* be staying in for the rest of the trip and Marissa is in the room right next door. "So?!" She bounces up and down in her heels as we walk through the lobby. She links her arm through mine. "Did you do it?"

"Do what?" I ask, knowing exactly what she means.

"You know what! You and Mr. Beckham?" She makes a circle with her index finger and thumb and sticks her other index finger through it to demonstrate what she means.

"No, Marissa!" I laugh.

"Seriously?" she asks. "Wow, I really thought he was going to make a move."

"Nope," I say without looking at her. I'm not a terrible liar, having learned the basics when I was in high school and trying to go to a party my dad would never let me go to, but I don't know how long I can keep it up if she keeps pressing it.

"Hmmm, well there's still time," she says as we walk into the conference room. There are only ten of us here in Miami, so the room consists of a long mahogany table and ten chairs. There's a very large spread of breakfast and lunch foods on the table and a bucket filled with bottles of champagne in the back. There's a whiteboard in the front and a sign with the words *Welcome, Beckham Securities!* on it.

"I think if he was going to, he would have before all of you got here, don't you think?" The words fly out seamlessly.

"I'd say yes, if not for the fact that he's literally staring at you right now like he wants in your panties." I look at Marissa and notice that she's not looking at me and I refuse to look at Wes in fear that anyone who catches us sharing a look could see the chemistry.

"Marissa..." I trail off.

"Fine," she says waving me off like she's done with the topic—*though I assume not forever*—before she slides her blazer off. "We decided on the flight down here that we are going to this club tonight. Brendan already booked us a table with bottle service. We have dinner and then we are going to pregame in one of our rooms and be out by ten or eleven?" She stands up to get some food before I have a chance to respond.

The thought of going out in Miami without Wes makes me antsy. Not because I'm nervous but because I'm just more comfortable with him than I am with anyone else here other than Marissa. I *want* to spend time with him. A few moments later, she sits back down and points to her plate offering me something from it. "I also re-downloaded my Tinder; I think I need a vacation fuck. It really helps clear my head," she says with a chuckle. "Do you use dating apps?"

"Not anymore," I tell her honestly. After college, I had a short-lived affair with this app called *Our Circle*—which was supposed to be better than Tinder. It left me with two awful first dates and my vow to avoid dating apps like the plague.

"How else do you expect to get laid?" she says as she takes a bite of a mini croissant.

By working for a man that's obsessed with me?

"Do we really want to get drunk on our first night here?" I ask, already trying to come up with a way to get out of this.

"Why do you think we don't have to be at our first meeting until eleven tomorrow? They want us to bond!"

"By blacking out?"

She giggles and taps my nose. "You're coming out. It'll be fun!"

Fuck. Wes is not going to love this idea.

The day goes by quickly and pretty soon I am getting ready to meet up with the rest of the team to go out. Wes was in business mode for the most of the day and since most of the eyes were trained on him as he went over some of the sales plans for the remainder of the year as well as how we'd start next year, it kept his eyes from lingering on me for too long.

I'm putting on a pair of gold hoops when my phone rings with a Facetime call and I'm not surprised to see that it's Wes. I immediately open it and prop it up against the mirror in the bathroom.

"Hi."

"Fuck, I miss you." I turn to look at him and notice that he's already dressed for dinner in a navy suit and he looks so fucking good. "Not being able to touch you all day was just as tortuous as I thought it'd be." He pulls his drink to his lips. "Stay the night with me tonight; no one will know."

I'd pulled my hair into a high ponytail after I learned my lesson with the humidity yesterday, and I spray a bit more hairspray to make sure it doesn't move. "I'll think about it." I scrunch my nose. "It all depends on how easily I can get away from everyone and if Marissa wants to have a late-night debrief after we get back, because…" I lean down so I'm eye level with my phone. I have some news you may not love."

"Oh, about you all going out tonight?" He rolls his eyes.

"You know about that?"

"I know everything."

I cock my head to the side. "How?"

"Chris overheard some of the guys talking." He shrugs.

"Sorry you weren't invited."

He laughs. "I wouldn't go even if I was invited. I try to keep the line very clear that I'm your boss and not your friend."

"Oh, is that the message you're sending me as well?"

"I'm not sending you any messages, Raegan. I speak them loud and clear. Do you need a refresher?"

His voice is low and vibrates through me. I shake my head, because all his refresher would succeed in doing is turning me on while there's nothing he could do about it. "Maybe I could get out of going..."

He shakes his head. "Baby, I think you should go. You'll have fun."

"I'd have more fun with you."

He smiles that lethal grin and I press my thighs together, willing away the ache that's building between my legs. "Undoubtedly, but it's good for you all to hang out. It's good for morale when you all get along."

"What are you going to do tonight?" Thoughts of Lily and Claire both trying to flirt their way into his bed tonight come into my brain before I can stop them and when I hear him chuckle, I realize I'm staring off into space with a scowl on my face.

He rubs his thumb over his lip. "Not whatever you're thinking."

"I..." I try to come up with a lie and fail. "I just know that there's a lot of trouble that two guys can get into in Miami. Something tells me Chris won't let you stay in tonight. He might want to get together with Claire and her friend." I scrunch my nose and try to ignore the annoyance flowing through me.

"I wouldn't do that and Chris wouldn't suggest it. There's also not a lot of trouble a guy will get into when he's committed to one woman." He frowns. "I'm sorry you don't have a lot of experience with a man like that."

Are you surprised by this? He basically told you he was ready to knock you up. Do you really think he'd go fucking random girls on a work trip that you're also on?

He wouldn't even if you weren't here, my subconscious immediately perks up.

"You're really kind of amazing, you know that?"

"I know." He smiles.

"Ugh." I scoff, but a smile pulls at my lips "You had to ruin it." There's a knock on the door and I look at it somewhat woefully before turning back to the phone. "That's Marissa. I have to go."

He nods. "Have fun. Not too much."

Chapter THIRTEEN

WES

"IF YOU'RE JUST GOING TO BE SEXTING HER ALL NIGHT, why didn't you just stay in with her?" Chris says from next to me where we're seated at the hotel bar. We'd contemplated going out but after Chris realized I wasn't serving as any kind of wingman for him tonight, we decided not to go far.

I look up from the sexy text from Raegan about how much she wants to run her tongue over my piercings when she sees me later and I turn towards Chris. "Because this is what they do on these trips, I don't want her to feel alienated from her coworkers."

"Even the one that wants to sleep with her?" He asks without pulling his eyes from the television that's showing highlights from a game from earlier.

"She doesn't want him." While I admit the thought of Liam trying to flirt with her all night doesn't sit particularly well with me, I trust her. *Not to mention, she barely even wanted to go.*

"Well, look at you. I can remember a time that it would have driven you crazy knowing some guy was hitting on your girl. Look who's grown up," He jokes and I cringe thinking about the jealous asshole I used to be and while it can flare up from time to time, I really have to be triggered.

"I definitely had a jealous problem, but I think I also dated women that exploited that. They got off on me being jealous so they did things they knew would bother me." I pull the whiskey to my lips, thinking about how different Raegan is. "Raegan isn't like that. She's just so…genuine."

"You sure you're not just a little bit enamored with her? You know the thrill of something new and exciting and forbidden? Young girl, she works for you, she's also a little obsessed with you. You're old enough to be her father?" He waves his hand to say et cetera. "You guys are like a walking psych study."

"You would know, you took it twice."

"There's a special place in hell for people who put mandatory classes at eight a.m. on Fridays." He groans. "But, Wes, I'm serious, and also, I thought you just wanted to fuck her. You're acting like this is more than that." He drains the contents of his glass.

"It is more than that."

He scratches his jaw before running a hand through his hair. "It's been a week."

"Okay? When you know, you know."

He sighs and waves over the bartender to order us both another drink. "Okay and what exactly do you know?"

"That being with her feels good and I want to continue whatever this is." I stare down at a picture of her that I'd taken while she was cuddled against me in bed. I wish like hell I was there with her now.

"And you're going to deal with HR?"

"Yes."

"Before you get caught, Wes," he says in a warning tone.

"I know."

"That means stop feeling her up at the office until you do. There's also a very big chance that she won't be allowed to be your assistant once you tell them and that's if they don't push to let her go."

"I'm not going to let them fire her."

"I'm also concerned about what they're going to do to you."

"They're not going to move to fire *me*."

"Probably not, but we have a board for a reason and they may make your life difficult for a while."

"I'll handle it."

I expect more pushback but when I look at him, he's looking down at his phone and then he looks at me with a smug grin. "So, maybe we should just go over there."

"Go over where?"

"Where your girl and the rest of the team is," he says waving a hand towards the bartender and signaling for the check.

"Why would we do that?"

"Because I was invited." He shrugs and I wonder who in the hell he's friends with enough to be invited to hang out with them.

"Oh, for fuck's sake, who are you sleeping with?"

"No one," he says as he gives the bartender his credit card. "I'm fun unlike you, so I'm invited sometimes when they go out."

"And you rarely go. Why now?"

"Maybe I want my buddy to be able to hang out with his girl." He slings an arm around my neck.

I move out of his grasp and shoot him a look. "It's not like I can touch her. Try again."

"Fine." He rolls his eyes. "I may be engaging in a mild flirtation with Miss Collins."

I groan. "Of course, you are. Do not sleep with her."

"Why not? She's insanely hot and she is one of the few people that you have screamed at that hasn't quit. I like that." He signs the receipt. "But don't do that shit again."

"Because I don't want you to slip up and tell her about me and Raegan," I tell him, ignoring the part about reprimanding her.

He snorts as he gets up and begins walking away like he's already decided we're going. "She's friends with Raegan, you don't think she already knows?"

"No, I told Raegan she couldn't tell anyone."

"Hardly seems fair; you told me."

"Because who are you going to tell? I don't know Marissa well enough to not go telling my business to the whole company."

We make it to the lobby and Chris crosses his arms. "You're being kind of annoying and it's killing my buzz. I'm going. Are you coming or not?"

Obviously, I go because despite the fact that I can't touch her, I can see her.

I don't tell her I'm coming and when we get to the club and the table in the private area. I take a moment to drink her in before we get to the table. She's sitting between Marissa and another girl on one side of a U-shaped booth, her head tilted back in laughter and she looks so fucking gorgeous I can't take my eyes off of her. Her top ties around her neck, highlighting the slope and making me want to run my tongue along the skin. A nudge from Chris breaks my stare and we walk the remaining steps to the table.

"Funny seeing you all here," Chris says and a few of the drunker people cheer. A few even clap as they begin pouring us drinks from the bottle of vodka in the center of the table. Marissa shakes her head as she tries to hide her smile behind her hand and when my eyes land on Raegan she shifts in her seat and avoids my gaze. "Mind if we join you?" he asks, and Brandon, one of the guys on the fast track for a promotion, stands up to grab a chair from an adjacent table for me to sit while Chris squeezes between Marissa and a guy from the tech department. I nod at Brandon who is definitely a bit of a kiss-ass, but he is good at his job.

I can tell the entire team isn't here, making me wonder if some people didn't come or if they're somewhere else in the club and I have to say I'm grateful I don't see Liam anywhere. I slide the chair on the side closest to Raegan and her eyes finally meet mine.

"I thought you don't usually come out with the team?" She asks, leaning over the girl that's seated between us due to the volume of the club.

"I guess Chris was invited. I tagged along just to make sure everyone was behaving themselves." I run my gaze over her and her eyes widen before she pans the group and I can see the relief on her face when she realizes no one is paying attention.

The girl between us, Beth, a married woman, who from what I've observed doesn't act quite so married on these trips, taps Raegan's leg. "I'm going to see what's taking Liam so long with the bottle of tequila." She's up and out of the area within seconds and I take her seat without hesitation, putting me right next to Raegan. She turns to me and raises an eyebrow.

"Have you enjoyed your time in Miami so far?" she asks. Marissa is sitting next to her but she's not paying attention at all. In fact, no one is.

"As a matter of fact, I am. Time of my life," I tell her and I hope she reads between the lines that I'm referring to the time I've spent with her over the last day and a half.

It seems she does because that delicious pink I love, coats

her cheeks and she turns to the center where all the drinks are. "Do you want a drink?"

"Vodka's my only option?" I chuckle. I rarely drink vodka, having spent the better part of my twenties drinking it like it was water.

She leans over and picks up a bottle of Jameson and I shake my head at that as well. She giggles. "Are you a whiskey snob?"

"Maybe a little." She laughs and it makes my heart beat a little faster that I amuse her even when she's trying to not be affected by me.

"I love your laugh," I tell her, my voice low and I'm grateful that no one is paying attention to us. It's as if we are in our own little world, and though she's not looking at me, I can tell she wishes she was. She spins the ring that she wears on her middle finger and lets out a sigh.

"Wes..."

I don't even try to stop the smile from pulling at my lips hearing my name fall from hers. "Yes, honey?"

Goosebumps pop up all over her arms and when she pulls her drink to her lips, I think she's about to say something when Beth and Liam return to the table.

"Who wants a shot?!" Beth squeals.

Liam's eyes immediately go to Raegan and then flit to me, and I can sense that he's annoyed at seeing her next to me.

"Didn't realize you guys were coming out tonight?" he asks me before he turns his eyes to Chris.

Chris, who has no patience for any passive-aggressive bullshit ever, chuckles. "I'm sorry, aren't you all using the company card to pay for all of this?" He spins his finger in a circle. "Why wouldn't we be here? He's paying for it." He points at me and I can hear the giggle from a few of the girls including Marissa. "We can't have fun too?"

Liam gives what looks like a fake smile before sitting down across from me and Raegan though his eyes are still fixed on her.

"So, who wants a shot?" Beth repeats as she claps her hands. She opens the bottle and begins pouring multiple shots before looking at me. "Mr. Beckham, you have to take a shot with us!"

"One." I hold up a finger.

"You drink tequila?" Raegan asks with a giggle. "And I'm just now learning this?" She says it low enough for only me to hear, careful not to alert everyone that she's saying something only to me.

"Socially."

"Hmmm," she says. "Does it make your clothes fall off?" She asks just as Beth hands me a shot, although I think she's too drunk to catch what Raegan said. I look at Raegan from over the tops of my glasses and she beams up at me like there's no one else in the room. I want to tell her that *she* makes my clothes fall off better than any alcohol ever has.

The group of us take the shot and I'm hyper-aware of how Raegan licked the salt from her hand just before she downed her shot making me wish we were alone so I could have licked the salt off of *her. Fuck, I want to get her out of here and back to our room.*

I don't know how much time goes by where Raegan and I are seated next to each other but not saying anything to each other. I don't miss the way her hand drags against my thigh every few minutes, *accidentally.* There are even more times that her arm bumps against mine and another time that she turned her back completely to me to talk to Marissa where her ass rested against my thigh. Her top is backless *again,* and I try to keep my gaze off of the toned, bare skin.

It's almost as if she wants to make sure she's always touching me even when we aren't talking or even looking at each other. Like she wants to touch me even when she can't.

About an hour later, I pull out my phone preparing to text her that I'm planning to make my exit and maybe she should join me when Liam stands up, his dark eyes staring at Raegan.

"We're out of vodka, I'm going to get another bottle. Rae, you want to come with me?"

I can feel Raegan, who's mid-conversation with Marissa, stiffen next to me and turn her gaze up to Liam who's looking down at her, and I absolutely fucking hate that he's trying to use some bullshit psychological power dynamic on her right now.

"What, you need help?" Chris jokes, and a few of the people laugh with him because *again, kiss asses.*

"No." He chuckles. "I just wanted to chat for a minute," he says and I realize that he's a bit drunk and based on what I know about Raegan, she is not.

"Sure, yeah." She smiles before getting up and I miss the feeling of her pressed up against me.

The second she's gone, I'm instantly irritated because why the fuck am I here? I never go out with my team and now I'm here forced to witness some asshole hit on her when I know she's not interested. If I were back at the hotel, I'd be none the wiser to any of this until she got back to my room and told me. *I know she would tell me everything, I'm not worried about her keeping anything from me. But now I'm here and have to watch it?*

I could easily text her and have her meet me in a bathroom or a dark corner of the bar, but it's risky and there are multiple people here that could catch us. Neither one of us is ready to go public at this very moment and I'm not about to get us caught because I'm jealous over some guy I know she doesn't want. And yet, I flex my fist trying to temper the urge to hit him in the face.

I don't want him, Wes. I can practically hear her voice.

"I love Liam to death, but can he give it a rest?" I hear Marissa say just before she tips back another shot. "She's not interested," she sings and Chris looks at me from across the table with a look as if to say, *you hear that? Relax.*

But I can't. Raegan is fucking uncomfortable, and hell, so am I. I look out into the main area and spot her immediately at the bar. I can't make out her body language or her facial expressions but he's standing far too close to her for my liking.

"I think I'm going to head out," I announce to everyone, most of whom are too intoxicated to care. Still, I hear an, "A*wwww no!*" And a few variations of, "*Damn, already?*"

Marissa turns away from Chris to look at me. "Now?"

"Yeah, I have some work to do, and I want to get up early but you guys have fun." I stand and make my way out of the section. I do my best to avoid the bar area because I don't want to get Raegan's attention even though I want nothing more than to stake my claim in front of that asshole. But we decided to wait a month and I care more about telling HR first before exploding all over some asshole that works for me and letting him use that shit against me out of spite over the fact that Raegan chose me over him.

I make it outside and let out a breath, already feeling better being out of that club despite the irritation still in my veins over Liam hitting on my girl.

They were just talking. She doesn't want him.

I take a step towards the valet when I hear a voice behind me. "You were just going to leave without saying goodbye?" I turn around and see Raegan by herself, her arms crossed over her chest, and one eyebrow raised, her face laced with irritation. "To me?"

"Baby—" I start and she shakes her head.

"Nope, you can't sweet talk your way out of this. You were just going to leave?" She takes a step closer to me and gives me those eyes that make me want to drop to my knees and give her whatever she wants. "I didn't know what to say. I didn't have a reason to say no," she says, referring to Liam.

"I know."

"Please don't be upset with me."

I shake my head. "I'm not."

"Then why are you leaving?"

"Because I can't claim you here and it's making me crazy and unless you want me to shoot our plan to hell, I need to leave. I can't watch some guy flirt with you like you don't belong to me." I take a step towards her so I'm right against her. "And make no mistake, Raegan, you do belong to me." I reach between us and cup her between her legs gently and she gasps, her eyes flitting around us before falling back on me. "This belongs to me." She's wearing a pair of pants that make her ass look so fucking amazing, but at this moment, I wish she were in a skirt or a dress for me to move her panties to the side and sink my fingers inside of her.

"I know I do. I told him I have a boyfriend."

My hand slides away from between her legs as I stare at her in somewhat shock. "You did?"

She tilts her head to the side. "Well...don't I?" She shrugs and looks around us before looking up at me. "I mean you did say you wanted to have a baby with me eventually, so I took that to mean you're kind of my boyfriend," she says with a hint of sarcasm.

I smile at her, a little at a loss for words at the idea of her calling me that. "I'm going to get a car and I'm going to wait until you're ready to leave. You should probably wait thirty or so minutes so we're not leaving at the same time."

She nods. "You'll wait for me?"

I cup her face and brush my lips gently over hers for the first time since this morning. "Of course, I don't want you trying to get back to the hotel by yourself."

She nods and gives me a smile before she disappears back into the bar.

Chapter FOURTEEN

Raegan

"BOYFRIEND?!" MARISSA GRABS MY ARM AND PULLS me away from the table before I even make it back there. "Wh—what? Did you just make that up to get him to back off? Tell me fast. Or do I need to corroborate this story? I haven't answered Liam's text yet." She brings a glass filled with a clear liquid to her lips, but I pull it away from her mouth and towards my nose to smell it hoping it's water because she's drunk quite a bit tonight.

"Marissa, maybe you should slow down. You're going to be hungover tomorrow." She's wearing a gold strapless dress that practically makes her brown skin glow against it, a fact that Christopher Holt must also notice because his eyes haven't left her once all night. "Are you going to sleep with Chris?"

She turns her eyes towards the table and then back to me. "I don't know. Maybe." She puts her hands over her eyes and then groans. "Okay, I'm going to tell you something but don't freak out."

I narrow my eyes at her. "Oh God, what?"

"I've slept with him before."

"What?!"

She puts a hand up. "Before I worked here!" She lets out a nervous laugh and puts a hand over her eyes, "and a few times since I worked here."

"Wow, oh my god." I'm grateful I'm more sober which allows me to do some basic math easily. "Wait. You've worked here three years and wasn't his divorce just *recently* finalized?"

"I didn't know at the time." She huffs. "I met him at a wedding. His childhood best friend was marrying my college roommate and we were both in the wedding blah blah blah. I get a little slutty at weddings; I don't want to talk about it. His wife was not there and I don't remember seeing a ring but I was very drunk. Nevertheless, he obviously did not tell me that."

"Okay, so...how did that lead to you working here?"

"Coincidence? Karma?" She snorts. "I don't know. I got the job before I even realized he worked here. I slept with a married man; he didn't exactly give me his credentials." She scoffs. "It makes me cringe to think about. I am a girl's girl!"

"I know." I rub her arm.

"Please don't think less of me."

"I don't!"

"Okay good. That's why I never told you or *anyone* that works here. I felt so ashamed after I found out. Imagine running into the guy who was the best sex of your life on your first day of work only to find out he's your married boss." She drains the rest of her glass and sets it on a nearby table. "Then Beckham screamed at me. Told you my day sucked." She winces. "He told me he was leaving her and then everything got so complicated and then his wife actually found out about me and it was such a mess. So, I went to Paris. I fled, because…I fell for a married man. But I ended it. I told him we were done until he was completely single. No bullshit separation either. I stayed away for a while and now…"

"Now, he's single and obviously very into you." I nod toward him and I notice him staring at us from the table. "You guys are definitely getting back together. He hasn't been able to take his eyes off of you all night."

"Okay enough about me. Boyfriend?"

"Okay. Since we are trading secrets…"

"Oh my God!!" She cheers and points at me. "I knew it. I knew it, knew it, knew it!" She taps my nose three times each time she says it. "He's so down bad for you. I knew I wasn't crazy." She slaps my arm. "How could you not tell me?! Since when?"

"Umm, the holiday party?" I answer weakly.

Her mouth drops open. "I die! Of course. Oh my God. I need to know everything."

I chuckle and put a hand over my eyes. "Please don't tell anyone." I'm hoping since she shared something she didn't want getting out, she'll keep my secret too.

"I swear! Wait, does Chris know?"

"Yes, but only him."

"I love this so much. I knew I was right! Well go, what are you still doing here? Didn't he leave?"

"He's outside waiting for me, but he didn't think we should leave at the same time."

"Oh, who cares? Everyone's drunk." She waves me off. "But if you want, we can go by the table for you to say goodbye." We start walking away from the crowded dance floor and towards our table when she stops again. "Wait! How is it?" I give her a look not understanding what she means and she groans in frustration. "The sex, Rae!"

"Oh! It's..." I bite my bottom lip thinking about how to describe what Wes Beckham is like in bed. "Unreal."

"Ugh, love that for you. He seems like he'd be good in bed even if he is a grumpy asshole half the time."

After saying goodbye, I'm back outside and moving towards the car Wes is waiting in when I feel a hand on my arm and a gentle tug. "Rae."

I turn around and I'm faced with Liam *again*.

This guy cannot take a hint. He wasn't at the table when I left, so maybe he just wants to say goodbye?

"Hey, what's up?"

"They said you were leaving. You're going by yourself?" he asks as he slides his jacket on.

"Ummm," I stammer, trying to come up with an answer. If I say yes, he'll undoubtedly offer to come with me and if I say no, he'll wonder who I'm leaving with. *Fuuuuuck.* "I'll be fine," I say not answering his question.

"It's late."

"It's Miami. It's never *late* here. It's midnight, so basically seven-thirty." I laugh.

"Still, I was thinking about leaving anyway. I'll go with you."

"Liam, I'm totally fine to go by myself."

"Okay? So, we can't share an Uber to the same place?" he asks and I can hear the accusation in his voice. I don't know what to say to that and even though it would create a huge problem, I really wish Wes was here. I don't say anything so he continues. "Look, I know you just told me you have a boyfriend because I was coming on a little strong and I'm sorry for that. I really like you and I hate that I've made you so uncomfortable." I don't say anything because I don't know what to say. "You're just so...beautiful," he starts and I realize now that he's even more intoxicated than he was when I talked to him earlier.

"I do...have a boyfriend."

"My Uber is here." He doesn't acknowledge what I say as he points behind me and starts walking towards the car. He reaches for my hand and I take a step back.

"Liam..." I let out a sigh. "I understand you're drunk, but you need to stop."

"Stop what?" He stares at me like he can't understand why I'm annoyed with him.

"Everything good, here?" I hear from behind me and then I see Wes in my periphery taking a step towards Liam and in front of me. Instantly, my heart flutters in my chest.

"I thought you left," Liam says.

"You didn't answer my question." He gives Liam a look. "You feeling okay?"

"Fine. Rae and I were just leaving." He points towards the car. "You ready?"

"No." I shake my head.

"Sounds like she's not ready." Wes crosses his arms in front of him. "I thought I advised you to flirt with my assistant on your own time."

"We're at a bar in Miami, it is—"

"Nope, you're still on a work trip," he interjects as he takes a step closer to Liam and I wonder if he's about to expose us. "I am not going to tell you again."

Liam looks at me and then back to Wes and then back to me, shooting me a glare. "Boyfriend, huh?"

"I don't know what you're implying, but I would tread lightly." Wes steps completely in front of me, blocking me from Liam's view. "Or we can have a talk with Human Resources when we get back about your insubordination."

He shakes his head before he gets in the car and pulls away from the front of the club.

I barely have a chance to register that I'm moving before I'm in the backseat of Wes' car and in his lap. "Are you okay?"

I nod as we pull away from the club. "Yes."

"I wanted to get out the second he approached you but I was trying to let you handle it, but it seemed like he was not getting it."

I shake my head. "He wasn't. He thought I made up the fact that I have a boyfriend."

"What a dick."

I rest my head on his shoulder, trying my best to get closer to him. "I hate that you couldn't tell him to back off because I'm yours."

I feel him harden beneath me and he tightens his hold on me. "Believe me, me fucking too." He guides my lips to his, sliding his tongue into my mouth and dragging it against mine. "You're coming to my room."

"Yes."

"And you're staying the night."

"Okay," I whisper, and he chuckles against my mouth.

"Wow, no pushback?"

"If I had just watched a woman hit on you for half the night, I wouldn't want you out of my sight either."

Wes must have a great sense of direction because even with me in his arms, my legs wrapped around his waist, and my mouth attached to his, he manages to get us out of the elevator and to his door. I don't stop grinding against him as I try to get some friction against my pussy. He gets us into his room and pins me to the wall, driving his cock against my center.

"Wes," I moan.

He licks a trail up my neck and I shiver in his arms. "Yes, baby?"

"Get me naked, *please,*" I beg. "I need you so badly."

"Fuck, I need you too." He reaches behind me and unties the bow behind my neck before pulling it off over my head with one hand all while holding me up with the other and it just reminds me how strong he is. "I wanted to touch you all fucking night. I hated that someone else could do so freely while I had to restrain myself." He says as he sets me on my feet.

"I only ever want you to touch me." I tell him. He said he wasn't mad and I don't think he is, but I can see he's worked up and the possessive jealousy written all over his face. His eyes are dark and his lips are pulled into a frown.

"Take off your pants." He tells me and I do as he says, taking them off and letting them pool on the floor leaving me only in a pair of red barely there silk panties. He gets on his knees in front of me and nuzzles his face against my sex, pressing his lips to my clit through the fabric and my knees buckle.

"Wes."

"Mmmhmm? Fuck, you smell good." I look down just as he's yanked the fabric to the side and dragged his tongue through my slit.

I squirm under his tongue, my body already wound up from dry humping in the car all the way back to the hotel. "Wes, give me your dick. *Please*. I need it."

I run my fingers through his hair as he laps at me a few times before he stops suddenly and I gasp at the loss of contact. He slides my panties down my legs and my toes curl with anticipation of what's to come based on the way he's staring at my pussy. My eyes flutter shut when he opens me up with two fingers, my body preparing for that sinful tongue flicking against my clit when I feel a sharp sting coupled with a resounding smack.

"Wes, oh my God!" My head jerks down to where he's kneeling between my legs. "Fuck me."

"Not yet." He says as he rubs his fingers over my clit gently. "Not until we are clear on who you belong to."

"We already talked about this." I look down, raising an eyebrow at him. I cup his chin in my hand and brush my thumb over his lips. "I belong to you."

"Do you?"

I roll my eyes and let them flutter closed when I feel his two fingers gently pinch my clit. "You know I do."

The feeling of another smack on my clit makes me moan. "Tell me whose pussy this is." His voice, sexy and deep vibrates through me.

"Yours!"

He lays another smack on my wet flesh. "Yours, what?"

"Oh, God. Yours, Daddy. You know it's yours."

He starts to rub my clit in circles and I let out a sigh. "That's right. Make no mistake, Princess, I'm not angry with you. But I don't like having to watch another man touch what's mine. It will always drive me fucking crazy seeing another man touch *you*."

"I know. I hated it." I run my hand through his hair and scratch his scalp, trying my best to calm him. I can tell he's worked up and while it's hot to see this side of him, I don't want him thinking I want anyone but him. "Please fuck me."

I look down to see his eyes looking up at me, his bottom lip pulled between his teeth. "I wonder..." He trails off as he continues to rub two fingers over my clit. "If you can come like this." He lands another satisfying smack on my sex, this time more on my clit and I can feel the dull throb start to intensify.

"Daddy." I moan. "*Please.*" He smacks me again and my head falls back against the wall. "You're teasing me."

"Okay." He blows gently against my wet cunt and I shiver at

the coolness against my hot flesh. "I'll make you a deal." He rubs my clit gently.

"Oh God, another deal." I choke out and he chuckles. "What is it?"

"I'll give you twenty seconds to rub this pretty little pussy all over my tongue." He spreads my legs and sends one over his shoulder. "If you don't come, we're going to try my little experiment and I'm going to spank you until you come all over my hand."

Fuck. "What if I do come? Then what do I get?" I breathe out.

"Whatever you want," he tells me.

"I think you're underestimating how good your tongue feels on my clit," I tell him as I press my sex to his mouth. I run one hand through his hair before tugging it gently to get him where I want him and begin rocking my hips against him. His tongue doesn't move how it usually does, only flicking every few seconds. And at this angle and on one leg, it's a little difficult to make myself come against him. He wants me to do all the work. *He did this on purpose.*

Just as I finally find a rhythm against him, he pulls back and looks up at me with those gorgeous blue eyes and a smug grin on his shiny full lips. "Times up."

"So, you don't want me to come, is that what you're saying?" I glare at him, knowing that making me come is already high on Wes Beckham's favorite things to do.

"There will be plenty of time for you to come on my tongue later." He opens me up again and smacks me three times in succession causing me to let out a sound somewhere between a squeal and a moan. "But I shouldn't let you come at all after all the teasing you did today." He presses his hard body against mine, dragging his finger down my body and between my legs to massage my clit. "At one point, I had to make the active decision to stop looking at you because every move you made was turning me on." He drops his lips to my neck. "One look and you get me hard."

He lifts me into his arms and carries me to the bedroom. Within seconds, he's seated on the bed and I'm across his lap, my body so wound up with the need to come. There's something so erotic about the fact that I'm completely naked and lying across his lap while he's fully clothed and my pussy throbs at the sexiness of it. He smacks one of my ass cheeks first, followed by the other. "I'm going to spank you for every time you teased me."

"I didn't do it on purpose!" I whine, even though I *definitely* did.

"Oh? I think that's a lie. I do remember quite a few sexy texts throughout the day and more than a few times you brushed against me when I couldn't react." His voice is low and I can already feel him hardening beneath me.

"Those were"—he lands a smack on my ass—"accidents!"

"And the texts about wanting to suck my dick the second you saw me?"

"I thought you'd like it!"

"Oh, I did, Princess. I liked it so fucking much." He smacks me rapidly three times on each cheek before he brings my ass up higher and brushes his knuckles against my wet sex.

I let out a breath, wondering if he's going to spank me or finger me. "Touch my pussy, please."

"You're so wet. You like Daddy's spankings, don't you?"

"Oh God..." I moan because if this is where we're going, I'm going to come so fucking hard when it's time. "Yes!"

"Your squirming, baby. Are you rubbing your wet pussy all over my suit?"

"Oh fuck." He lands another smack on my ass before I feel one on my sex and I dig my fingers into the bed, trying to release some of the tension coursing through me. "Spank me until I come, please," I beg. "I want to come, I need to come. I can't..." I trail off. "Daddy, please!"

"Are you going to tease Daddy anymore?" I don't respond and he lands another spank on my cunt causing me to moan. "Answer me."

"N-no." I respond, though we both know that's a lie.

"Are you lying to me?"

"Yes…" I trail off, and in a flash, I'm on my back on the bed, my legs spread, and he's kneeling on the floor in front of me. I look down just in time for the sting of three fingers on my clit to vibrate through me. "Fuck!"

"Your clit is so fucking swollen." He growls. "God, look how pretty you are." He smacks me five times in rapid succession each time a little harder than the last. "Do you want me to stop?"

"No, keep going." I drag a finger into my mouth and bite down.

"You tell me if it's too much."

"It's not." I moan. "It's never too much with you."

"Fuck. Baby, do you need me to fuck you now?" He asks and when I look down, I see him pulling off his jacket.

"Spank me first," I tell him and I move up onto my elbows so I can watch, totally enraptured by the way he touches me. I note that he's been using his tattooed hand which just adds to how hot all of this is. My pussy is pink and wet and my clit is completely exposed from him spreading me open. I feel a level of vulnerability that I've never felt with anyone ever and it's making my heart start to pound in my chest. I've been with men for multiple years and no one ever made me feel the way Wes does. No one touched me or fucked me or kissed me like he does. Hell, no one even looked at me the way he does. No one made me feel as cherished or like I was the most special woman in the room.

Hell, the most special woman in the world.

"You're a fucking goddess, Raegan." He smacks me again.

"No matter what fucking happens, nothing is going to take you away from me. Do you understand me?"

"Yes!" I moan as I feel him rubbing my sex again.

I'm nearing the edge now, my clit tingling and pulsing with every smack on it. "Daddy, I'm so close," I whimper.

"Oh good, but you know you're not done after this, right? I'm going to fuck you so hard and so deep after this. Ride this pretty little pussy while you take Daddy's cock."

"Oh my God." I moan as he smacks me one final time and I go over the edge. And because Wes Beckham is a literal fucking god, he presses his lips to my sex to let me ride out the rest of the orgasm against those full lips.

I watch as he gets undressed, slowly pulling his pants off and unbuttoning his shirt all while his eyes are fixed on me. "Can I be on top?" I ask him and he raises an eyebrow at me. We haven't had sex with me on top because he's convinced I won't get off of him in time which will end with him coming inside of me.

"Raegan," he says as he gets on the bed and pulls me into his lap. "You know how you get when you're close to the edge. You toy with both of our resolves and don't want me to pull out."

"Please," I move in his lap to face him and wrap my legs around his back as I wrap my arms around his neck. I flutter my eyelashes at him and press a light kiss to his lips. "Just for a second."

He narrows his eyes at me. "Neither one of us can stop after a second."

I giggle as I wrap my hand around his dick and drag my thumb over the tip. "It's not my fault. You have such a perfect dick." I guide him closer to my opening, dragging it through my slit and he lets out a groan.

I don't know how it's already become an unspoken thing that we aren't ever going to use condoms. It's as if we've already crossed this line of intimacy and there is no going back. Like condoms somehow would make the sex less intense.

He grips my ass, lifting me up so I can slide down on him. "Does it make you feel good that you can get me to do whatever you want?"

"Yes." I smirk at him as I sink all the way down his length and squeeze when he bottoms out inside me. "I love that you'll do anything to make me happy."

"Fuuuuuck." He groans. "Anything," he whispers against my lips as we find a rhythm, our bodies moving together in perfect synchronization despite the fact that we've never had sex in this position.

"Will you take me on dates when we get back home?"

"Anywhere you want."

"Can we go shopping again?"

"In Paris?" he asks and I giggle against his neck as he thrusts in deeper, turning it to a moan. "Whatever you want, baby."

"I like the sound of that. How long do I get this special treatment?"

"For as long as you want."

Chapter FIFTEEN

Raegan

We got back from Miami Sunday night and despite the fact that I want to curl up in bed with Wes, Lucas came back this weekend. I want to see him and spend time with him and my dad. I'm sitting in Wes' car parked in front of my house, wishing we were ready for me to introduce him to my other two favorite guys so he could come in.

"You okay?" he asks, pulling my hand to his lips.

"Yes, I've just gotten accustomed to sleeping in your bed and I'm thinking about how I'm not going to tonight." I've never felt this attached to anyone this early on but being with him just makes me feel so good.

"You are welcome to come over later."

I give him an innocent smile. "Why don't you come here?"

He looks at me from over his glasses. "You want me to

meet your dad and your brother?" I can sense his nerves but I know he'd do it if I asked him to.

"No, but you could wait until they go to sleep and you can sneak in."

He snorts. "I am *not* sneaking into your father's house, Raegan."

A fantasy of us fooling around in my bedroom floats through my brain and I feel the space between my legs getting slick. "Why not!"

"Because…" He trails off. "Because I'm too old for that." He laughs and I roll my eyes.

"Fine." I lean across the console and rub a hand against his cheek. "I had fun in Miami."

"Me too."

Christmas is Wednesday, so *Beckham Securities* is closed this week. Wes and some of the senior team will be working tomorrow, but most of us are off, considering a number of us just came from Miami where we worked this past weekend.

"Will I see you before Christmas?"

"Christmas is three days from now, I would hope so. Besides, you need to get your gifts."

"Well, I already know what they are." I smile, recalling my impromptu shopping spree. Wes agreed to take them all home because I wasn't exactly sure how I'd explain almost a hundred thousand dollars worth of stuff I definitely did not have before I left for Miami.

"There are some you haven't seen yet."

"You bought me more stuff? Wes…" I trail off.

"You were a very good girl this year, so yes, I got you more things you haven't seen." He shoots me a look and just the mention of those two words makes me squirm.

"Tomorrow?" I ask and the excitement is already coursing

through me at the plan already in place for when we'll see each other again.

"Tomorrow, baby." He kisses me gently and then I'm out of the car.

It's fucking freezing here and my body is not happy after it briefly got acclimated to the warm temperatures of Miami. I enter my garage and through the door to a quiet house and I'm surprised I don't hear anything.

"Who's the guy in the car?" I hear my little brother's voice from behind me and I jump almost a foot in the air.

"Jesus! Don't do that!" I slap his arm. A moment later, the biggest smile finds my face and then I'm in his arms pulling him into a hug. "I missed you so much!" I squeeze him a little harder, happy to have one of my favorite people home. "You look good." I reach up and ruffle his hair. "This is a little long," I tell him as he waves my hand away.

Lucas was almost the spitting image of our dad, minus the facial hair and his blue eyes like mine and our mother's whereas our dads are brown, but he has the same dark hair and build and smile that always made me feel better.

"Don't avoid the question," he says as he takes a sip of his beer. "You got a boyfriend?"

"Sort of." I bite my bottom lip. "Well, yes, but it's new. I haven't even told Dad."

"Haven't told Dad what?" My dad walks into the kitchen and Lucas shakes his head at me as if to say *I was not trying to set you up.*

"I am seeing someone. It's new and I'm not ready for you guys to meet him yet, but soon." *My dad is pretty relaxed for the most part but I'm not sure how he'll take me dating someone two years younger than him.* I need to think about how I'm going to prepare him for that.

"Is that why you've been MIA?" he asks as he leans against one of the counters in our state-of-the-art kitchen.

"Well, I was in Miami for work, remember?" I'm definitely not going to lead with the fact that I work for Wes. That's information for later...*way later.*

"I mean before that. The weekend prior when you weren't here at all?" my dad asks.

"That was because of the snow. I was at my friend's house, remember?"

"Mmmhmmm." He goes into the living room and Lucas and I follow him. He drops to the couch, turning on the television and I sit next to him, sliding my shoes off. I'm exhausted from the trip, and I'll probably go to bed soon but I can hang out with them for a little while.

"Oh, Avery's here," Lucas says as he looks at his phone and heads to our front door.

"Has he been following her around all weekend?" I joke and I'm surprised when my dad doesn't respond. "Dad?"

"Oh sorry, what?" He looks at me. "Sorry, I was thinking about something." He shakes his head. "What did you say?"

"If Lucas has been following Avery around all weekend?" It's no secret that Lucas used to harbor a huge crush on Avery Summers for most of their middle and high school years. *Even when she had a boyfriend and he had a girlfriend.* I can remember so many nights when Lucas would come home hammered from a party and he'd be going on about how crazy he was about the girl that lived next door who was also his best friend. She's never had feelings for him to my knowledge and now he claims he's grown out of those feelings, but I don't buy it for a second.

"Hey, guys." Avery, who is probably one of the most beautiful people I've ever seen in real life, comes bouncing into the room full of energy just like she always does. I'm off the couch instantly and pull her in for a hug. I almost want to steal her away to my room and tell her all about Wes because she's the one person I could tell who would actually be super excited for me. Avery has always been supportive and my number one hype girl whenever it came to anything. But Lucas would probably have a fit if he couldn't be up under her for five seconds.

"Avery!" I squeal. "I'm so happy to see you!"

"Me too! They told me you were in Miami. I am so jealous! It's freaking freezing here."

"Oh yeah, it was great. I really love my job." *I also love sleeping with my sinfully gorgeous boss.*

"Hi, Theo." She waves towards my dad.

"Avery." He nods at her and I frown wondering why he's being so grumpy when he's usually the nicest guy in the world. I roll my eyes before turning back to Avery.

"We are going to grab a drink. Do you want to come with us?" Lucas asks me as he pulls his coat off of one of the bar stools in our kitchen.

I sigh and shake my head. "Guys, I am beat. I literally just got off a plane." *Not Wes' sexy private plane for the record which was annoying.* "I'm down for maybe tomorrow, but tonight I am so tired."

"Why are you so grumpy tonight?" I ask my dad from my side of the couch. I'd gone upstairs to change before deciding to watch a movie with my dad since Lucas is still out. When Lucas is home, they're usually glued to the television watching sports.

"I'm not," he answers, not pulling his eyes away from the

movie as he grabs some popcorn from the bowl between us. "Tell me about this guy."

"Don't change the subject."

"It's nothing, Rae. I'm good." I know exactly what his problem is. He's lonely and I fucking hate it. I want him to meet someone so badly. He's one of the best people I know and I wish he had someone to share his life with. He's barely dated since he and my mom divorced and that was almost six years ago.

I don't push it because, more than anything, I don't want him dwelling on it, so I let him change the subject. "I really like him." I wrap the fluffy blanket tighter around me. "I may even love him."

He mutes the television and looks over at me. "Love, huh? How long has this been going on?" He asks.

"Not long officially but...I don't know, maybe longer than either of us realized." I tell him honestly. Wes has been pretty candid about how he's had feelings for me for months and the more I sit with my thoughts, I believe I've had them as well.

He nods and crosses his arms over his chest. "Can I know his name?"

"Wes," I tell him and a smile immediately pulls at my lips, like it's the most natural reaction to saying his name.

"You're blushing."

I touch my cheeks and rub them, trying to soften the pink. "Sounds about right."

"Is it love, hon, or lust?"

I scrunch my nose, not wanting to talk about any kind of lustful feelings I have for Wes. "Can we not?"

"You're almost twenty-two. I'm not going to tell you how you feel but you don't want to rush into things."

"I know. We aren't." *Lies.*

My dad snorts and when I look at him, he's giving me a look that says, *yeah right*. "Raegan Marie, I know you better than you know yourself."

"Okay." I tilt my head to the side as if to say, *and?*

"You just let me know when it's time to meet this guy, okay?"

Chapter SIXTEEN

WES

I HAD ALREADY PLANNED TO TELL HUMAN RESOURCES everything when we got back to Philadelphia. I know the plan was to wait a month, but I'm not sure if Liam now has a hunch, and I don't need him running his mouth to anyone who would listen before I have a chance to come clean. Raegan is probably going to be irritated, but I'm being proactive. Nothing is going to change between now and a month from now except that I will probably be ready to ask her to marry me. I've never felt this way about anyone and nothing is going to stop me from being with her.

I'm not planning to announce to the entire company that I'm in a relationship with my assistant, but I also don't want to run the risk of getting caught. This is the perfect time with half the team out for the holiday and only senior leadership working. I have a plan and I am going to make it work.

I'm sitting in the office with Dana, our head of human

resources, and two members of the board, all three of them staring at me like I'm here to fire them.

"Thank you for letting me schedule this meeting. I know we all have things to do and want to get out of here as soon as possible for the holidays, so I'm going to make this very quick and hopefully, you all don't have too many questions." I clap my hands and pinch the bridge of my nose. "I am in a relationship…with Miss Graham." Dana's brown eyes widen and immediately she shuts her eyes like she can see the HR nightmare happening before her eyes.

"Mr. Beckham—" Pete White, one of the older members of the board, who looks like Santa Clause and reminds me of my father, *and often tries to act like it,* interjects but I put a hand up, stopping him.

"I know about the no fraternization policies—" I start.

"Do you?" Dana pushes her glasses to her head and purses her lips, not necessarily in judgment but in disappointment. "You know what this means."

I snap. "We are *not* firing her."

"Those are the rules," Dana replies.

"Make new ones," I growl, "or I'll find a new head of HR." I give her a pointed look and she actually pales slightly. I don't want to fire her, but if it's between her or Raegan there's zero contest.

Pete sighs. "Who else knows about this?"

"Chris. Liam Patterson may have a hunch, I'm not sure, but we need to talk about him anyway for an unrelated reason." And not just because he's an asshole that wants my girl, but I don't like how much he pressed her the entire trip. It makes me wonder how many of the girls he's slept with did so willingly or just so that maybe he'd leave them alone. *I do not like that.*

"You know what will happen if this gets out?" Dana asks.

"It's giving everyone carte blanche to engage in inappropriate behavior at their desks!" Pete says.

"No, that's not what I'm saying at all," I tell him. *Although, I will definitely still be fucking Raegan on my desk, regardless of this outcome.* "I'm saying that if someone comes to us in the same way that I am now and professes to be in love with someone, I expect us to do a little bit of due diligence before we fire anyone. I'm not talking about flings or sordid affairs. I'm talking about a genuine connection between two people that just so happens to both work here." I sigh and the words tumble out before I have a chance to stop them. "I fell in love with someone who also happens to work for me." The words feel foreign having not said them in years and while Raegan and I haven't technically been together for very long, I know that I've been in love with her for longer than the week it's been since we started this.

"In love?" Eliana Song, who hasn't said anything since the moment we sat down, speaks up. She's always quiet, but she's also very kind so I'm not surprised that she's not at all combative during this meeting like the other two. She tucks a strand of her black blunt bob behind her ear.

"Yeah." I smile at her. "I love her."

She blinks at me a few times before she leans forward. "Does she feel the same way?"

"Not the point," Dana interjects.

"That's absolutely the point," Eliana responds with a glare before turning back to me with a small smile as if to say, *well?*

"I don't know. I haven't told her yet. It's relatively new. I mean...I think I've been in love with her for a while, but our relationship is new."

Dana sighs and pinches the bridge of her nose. "What is the point of all of this?"

"Being honest? Because there may come a point where we won't be able to hide that we're together." *Maybe she could hide a ring but I don't know how she'd get away with hiding my baby inside of her.*

"So, you want us to rewrite the rules."

"Yes," I tell them. "I own the company and I still hold the majority share. Chris also has a vote and I'm sure you can guess the way he'll vote. I called you guys in here as a courtesy, but make no mistake, I will pull rank if I need to." I stand up, as it seems like they're reluctantly getting on board with my request. "I'm not going to have her sitting in my lap during board meetings and I'm not suggesting we put it in the monthly newsletter, but I'd like to be free to hold her hand when we walk in the office together." I point at the three of them. "Email me the updates when they're done."

Later that night, I barely register that someone has opened my garage door before Raegan appears in my kitchen. She drops her overnight bag, pulls her shoes off, and then launches herself into my arms, wrapping her arms and legs around me, and pressing her lips to mine.

"I missed you," she says between kisses as I walk us to the couch and sit with her straddling my lap.

I don't think anyone has ever been this excited to see me ever, and my heart feels the same level of excitement over having her back in my arms. "Hi, baby, I missed you too."

We've spent the majority of the past six days together and even longer if you count the weekend after the holiday party, so this is the longest we've gone without seeing each other since we first slept together. She pulls back to rub my jaw before pulling my glasses off my face, having learned that I don't typically like kissing her with them on.

"How was your day?" I ask her while I run my hands up her sides and begin stroking her back.

"Good. I went shopping for your Christmas present. You know how hard it is to shop for a man who has everything? I figured those days were behind me since my dad *also* has everything but alas, here we are." She rolls her eyes.

I shake my head. "You absolutely did not need to get me anything." I hold her tighter in my arms. "All I want is you."

"Okay, Mariah Carey, well I got you something else besides me." She rubs a thumb over my lips before kissing me again.

I pinch her side playfully and she giggles. "Hey, I didn't quote the full title."

"I am impressed you know the song."

"Everyone in the world knows that song. But," I start, "while we are on the subject, I do know something you can do for me for Christmas."

"Do *for* you, huh?" She runs her hands underneath my t-shirt and drags her nails over the skin. "That sounds like you want me to let you stick your dick in my ass."

I freeze, my dick rising beneath her and beginning to throb at the thought of being inside her tight little ass. I blink at her, at a loss for words before I choke out, "Yes. Absolutely, yes." I take a deep breath, trying to calm my dick down. "But that's not where I was going. Can we hold that thought for just one second?" I hold a finger up, and she laughs and nods.

No, fuck her ass first, and then tell her.

I ignore the thought, having promised to be honest with her always.

"I have to tell you something and I would like it if you wouldn't get mad at me."

She stiffens in my lap but she doesn't try to move. "Okay?"

I put my glasses back on and set my hands on her thighs

that are still placed on either side of me. "I'm so crazy about you, you know that?"

"I know."

"And this past week has been probably the best week I've had, maybe ever, but it's been the holidays and things have been more relaxed at the office. I'm not so naive to think that in the New Year when things go back to normal, keeping our relationship a secret won't be more difficult."

"Mmmhmmm." She narrows her eyes at me and I wonder if she knows where I'm going with this.

"I spoke with HR," I blurt out.

She crosses her arms over those delicious tits that are hidden by a loose sweater. I expect her to climb off my lap but she doesn't and I'm happy that she's taking this better than I thought she would. "Didn't we say we were going to wait a month?"

"Yes, and I know I went rogue, but Liam is a wild card, and anyone else who may have picked up on anything between us in Miami. I just wanted to get in front of it. I'm sorry."

"I wish you would have talked to me first. Is that how things are going to be between us? We make a plan and you just change it without talking to me first?"

"No." I shake my head and cup her face. "It won't be like that. This involves a lot of other things outside of you and me. I'm sorry. I didn't think you'd be on board and I had to think like the CEO."

"I suppose that's fair…" She trails off and when she turns to me a playful smile is on her lips.

I lean back against the couch and study her for a second. "How did you know?"

"Maybe when you have HR email you about the relationship with your assistant, make sure said assistant doesn't have access to your emails."

Well fuck. I point a finger at her. "You're not supposed to be working."

She winces. "Well, you see, I forgot to turn my *out of office* automatic reply on and it was labeled urgent, so it pushed it to the top and notified me."

I shake my head at her. "I'm sorry."

"I am impressed you told me this soon. I thought you were just going to wait a month."

"What? No." I shake my head. "That would require me having to lie to you and I'm not ever going to do that."

Her eyes get a little glassy and then she wraps her arms around me and lets out a sigh before she pulls back to look at me. "You're not actually this perfect, right? Can you just tell me what's wrong with you now, so I can be prepared?" I chuckle as I stand up with her in my arms to carry her out of the room when she gasps. "Oh my God!" She hops out of my arms and I realize she hadn't noticed the Christmas tree yet. "When did you do this?"

"I didn't do it. I had someone come set it up while we were in Miami."

"It's so pretty!" She stares up at the ten-foot tree trimmed with white lights, ivory ribbon, and gold balls with everything she got in Miami underneath it. She turns around and grabs my hand pulling me against her. "Next year, I want to do it together."

"So, I told my dad about you," Raegan says as she grabs my hand and laces our fingers. I'm sitting behind her in my very large bathtub with her back pressed against my chest. She'd insisted on a mountain of bubbles that come up to her neck so it's blocking my view of her pretty tits. I drag my other hand not laced with hers up her side and cup one of her breasts since I can't look at them.

"What did you tell him?" I can feel the tension in my bones at the thought of him not approving of me *or my age.*

"Not much. Just that I'm seeing someone and I really like him. And your name."

I squeeze her breast. "No other details?"

"No, I wasn't ready to tell him about your age or that you're my boss. I'm not sure if either will bother him."

I press a kiss to her shoulder. "What will happen if it does bother him?" Based on how Raegan talks about her father, I don't see him giving her any kind of ultimatum, but I would hate to be the cause of a rift in their relationship.

"I don't know. He may just need time to get used to it." She rests her head against my chest and tilts her head up to look at me. "Do you think your parents will like me?"

"They'll love you. What's not to love?" I ask her and I mean that. They may be a little concerned about how much younger she is but once they meet her, I know they'd fall in love with her instantly the same way I had.

The words come out so easily, I don't even notice until I realize she hasn't said anything. *Fuck. It's definitely too soon to say that even if I am starting to feel that way.*

"I hope so," she finally says and I hold her tighter to me. "So, I brought one of my vibrators with me."

The swift change in conversation has my cock turning to stone. "Did you say one of…" An image of a sexy toy box underneath her bed takes over my thoughts and soon I'm picturing her fucking a pink vibrator, her body slick with sweat and screaming my name as she climaxes.

"Well, yes, I have a few. For penetration, for my clit, for both at the same time, one that—"

"Okay enough," I chuckle. "The visuals are too much."

She turns around to face me and sits on top of my dick without letting me slide inside of her. She grinds herself a little on top of me and I grip her shoulders, giving her a scolding glare.

"Stop being a tease." She spins her hips in a circle and I feel myself slide through her slit. "Raegan, do you want to get fucked?"

"Yes." She drags her tongue across my lips. "In my ass though."

"Fuuuuuck." I groan as I let my head fall back.

"That's why I brought my vibrator. I thought it might help with it being my first time." She bites her bottom lip. "I'm a little nervous, but you'll be gentle, right?"

"Of course." She opens her mouth and immediately shuts it before letting her eyes float around the room nervously. "What is it?" Raegan is slowly getting more comfortable talking about sex but I know she's not totally there yet.

Unless she's on the brink of an orgasm, then who knows what she'll say.

"You mentioned…doing some things before you put your dick there."

"Yes." I squeeze her ass and push one of my fingers inwards, rubbing the hole before probing it gently. "You'll probably come so hard with my tongue in your ass while your vibrator hums against your sexy little clit."

Her eyes widen, her mouth drops open, and as her cheeks turn bright pink my dick pulses at how much I affect her. *How much we affect each other.* "Wes."

"I'll bet you squirt all over your little fucktoy." I run my fingers over her nipples, stroking them. "You think about me while you use it?"

"Yes. I used it last night in the shower and I thought about that night in Miami when you spanked my clit until I came."

Her swollen, slick clit, pink and hot comes to mind, and my mouth fucking waters. "Fuck, that was hot."

"Can you do that again?" She sounds less timid than she did a few moments ago and I'm happy she knows I'll give her whatever she wants.

"Baby, you know I'll do whatever you want."

She's on top of me, her mouth wrapped around my dick, muffling her moans as I fuck her sweet pussy with my tongue. She's already come twice and now I'm rubbing her orgasm into that puckered hole as I prepare to fuck her there. I slide my tongue upward towards it and she gasps, letting me fall out of her mouth. "Wes, oh my God." She tenses slightly and I rub my hand over one of her ass cheeks gently, trying to soothe her.

"Baby, relax." I reach next to me, rubbing my hand over the sheets until I find her toy and slide it between us against her clit and she squeals.

"Oh!" She cries out, and her body shakes on top of me. "I can't believe your mouth is…there," she whispers. "It feels so dirty." Her tongue circles the tip of my dick and flicks my piercing and my balls tighten.

"Do you like it?" I nibble the flesh of her ass gently as I turn up the intensity of her vibrator.

"Fuck. I love it. I love everything you do to me." She wraps her lips around my dick and slides down my entire length and pleasure shoots through me, hot and fast.

I take the hand off her ass and grab her hair, pulling it. "Take me out of your mouth. I don't want to come yet. I want to come in your ass." She moans, letting my dick fall out of her mouth but still gripping it tightly at the base. "You like when I pull your hair?"

"Yes, Daddy." She begins to run her hand up and down my dick.

"Give me another orgasm and then I'm going to fuck you so deep, Angel." I probe her asshole with one finger, followed by a second and she clenches around me. My dick is painfully hard at the thought of this tight hole wrapped around it and I pull them out, so I can rim her again.

"Daddy, I'm going to come," she whines and her whole body tenses as she rocks against my face while the vibrator is still nestled against her clit. "Oh my God, yes! I'm coming! Oh fuuuuck." She moans and then I feel her wetness all over my torso and I thrust my hips upwards thinking about her squirting all over me.

"Fuck." I moan as I rub a hand between us, feeling her slippery cunt rubbing against me. She climbs off of me and stares at my chest with so much lust and then she's on top of me.

"Fuck me, fuck me, *please,*" she begs as she rubs her finger through her cum all over my chest. She drags the finger across my lips, coating them with her juices and I hold it to my mouth licking them clean before licking my lips. She drags her tongue through it next, licking herself off of me before she rubs her tongue along my lips.

I pull away after no more than a second, needing to be inside her. "You are so fucking sexy. Turn around." I reach for the lube on the nightstand.

"No."

"No? Did you change your—"

"No." She shakes her head. "But I want to sit on it."

"Fuck yes." I squirt some lube in my hand and rub it up and down my dick, trying not to focus on how good it feels before I can even get inside her.

She turns around and I also rub it against her asshole and she shivers in my arms. "I'm so glad I'm doing this with you." I pull her hard against my chest and press my nose against her cheek. "Nothing has ever felt this right until now."

Her words hit me square in the heart and in my head and my dick, and all of them are screaming at me to tell her how much she means to me.

But I refrain. Not when I'm about to fuck her this way. No, I'll tell her after, while I make love to her sweet body, with my lips on hers. "Raegan," I murmur low in her ear. "Do you know how I feel about you?"

"I think so." She moans as I press two fingers to her clit.

"Good. I'm always going to feel this way." She gasps and I press the vibrator against her again. "Keep this on your clit." She nods as I lay on my back and I hold my dick against her puckered hole. "You ready?"

"Yes," she squeaks and I hear the nerves in her voice.

"Stop if it's ever too much, okay?" I rub a little more lube there.

"I trust you to make it better if it hurts."

"You do?" I push into her slowly just as she pushes back onto me. "Oh, fuck, baby, go slow."

"Oh my God, it actually feels…really good." She moans and I wish I could see her face. *Reminder to get mirrors for next time.*

She grabs my thigh with one hand for leverage and begins working me further inside her sweet little asshole. Pleasure clouds my vision as she rocks herself further down. I have both hands on her hips to make sure she doesn't go too fast but I feel her wiggling to get free. "Daddy, let me, *please*. I want to fuck you."

"You are, baby. I just don't want you to go too fast." My balls feel like they've gone numb by how much they're tingling and I groan when she lowers the vibrator, dragging it over them. "Fuuuuuck."

"Do you like that? Feeling the vibrator I fuck myself with on your balls?"

"Yes yes yes." I groan.

"Daddy?"

"Yes, princess?"

"I think I'm going to come again." She moans. She's still only about halfway down my length and I can't wait for her to be fully seated on my dick. "I want to wait for you though."

"No, you come for Daddy, now. I want to know how it feels for my girl to come with me inside her asshole."

She giggles. "You're so dirty."

"You love it."

It's not lost on me how many times we've both thrown that word around tonight and I can feel us both inching towards it. It doesn't matter that it's so soon—*though again, not really that soon when you count the six months I spent pining for her*—I'm fucking in love with Raegan Graham and I almost can't wait another second to tell her.

Wait. You're going to freak her out.

I stare up at the woman on top of me working my dick with her ass and I can tell she's chasing her climax because she's starting to get a touch more erratic with her moves. "Yes, oh my God, Daddy, right there." I reach around to hold the vibrator against her as both of her hands grip my thighs and she lowers herself all the way down.

"Oh my God!" She screams and I almost black out from the pleasure of my dick being completely inside of her ass. Her feet are planted firmly on the bed as she begins to move up and down on me, and I grip her hips helping her with each thrust.

"Fuck, that's good, baby. You're doing so good fucking me. You want my cum, don't you? You're going to milk all my cum out of me."

"Oh my God, yes. Yes, yes, yes," she chants. "I'm coming,

fuck." Her head falls back and I begin thrusting upwards a little harder as I chase my own orgasm.

"Come in my ass, Daddy, *please*." She moans and I fucking. lose. it. I come with a roar inside her and she gasps.

"Fuck fuck fuck. There, baby." I struggle to keep my eyes open but eventually they close and when I open them again, I feel her pulling off of me. I sit up, my body feeling looser and more relaxed than it's ever felt and I stare at Raegan whose back is still to me, but she's on her hands and knees now, panting. "Holy shit." The words come out gravelly and I clear my throat. "That was—"

She turns to me, her eyes the brightest shade of blue I've ever seen brought on by the tears in them. "Incredible." She bites her bottom lip as a smile finds her face. I move behind her, wanting a look at my cum inside her, and spread her cheeks slowly.

"Wes." I hear the slightest bit of apprehension in her voice, I'm guessing over being exposed to me this way.

"Just for a second. I just want to see." Some of it has started to slide out and I push it back inside. "I love seeing my cum inside of you. I can't wait to see it leak out of your pussy."

I carry her to the bathroom, where we clean ourselves up in relative silence before we are back in bed, her body resting on top of mine. Neither of us has spoken for a while and I assume she's drifted off to sleep when she stirs.

"Wes," she murmurs and I wonder if she's in between being awake and asleep because her words are slightly slurred.

"Yes, honey?" I've been stroking her hair for the last few minutes but I stop as I wait for her to answer.

"I'm really happy." The room is dark so I can't see her but I feel her move and then she presses a kiss to my chest.

"Me too, baby."

"Will we always be this happy?"

"In every lifetime."

Chapter SEVENTEEN

Raegan

One Month Later

JANUARY FOURTEENTH, ONE OF MY FAVORITE DAYS of the year, *my birthday.* I slept at my house last night, but Wes mentioned having plans for us tonight, and I'm so excited. I also strategically planned to tell my dad more about Wes today and maybe facilitate an introduction when he picks me up because who can get mad at a girl on her birthday?

Like always, my dad is taking Lucas and me to Aspen this weekend, so we aren't doing much today, especially since I told my dad I had plans with my boyfriend. It's almost seven when I make my way downstairs preparing to tell my Dad about Wes.

"Oh, Dad!!" I say as I make it to the main floor.

"In my office!" he calls out and when I make it to the door, I see him staring at his computer. "There's the birthday girl." He smiles as he turns away from the screen. "You look beautiful. I assume you're not coming home tonight?" He raises an eyebrow at me. He's gotten used to me not sleeping here at least two nights a week and I'm surprised he hasn't really pressed me about meeting Wes.

"Correct, and I thought...maybe it's time for you to meet him?" I fidget with my hands, suddenly nervous even though I know if he can get past his age, he'll love Wes. We are going to hold off on telling him I work for Wes though. For now, he thinks he just works somewhere else in my building but not for my company.

"Oh? Finally, I get to meet this man that has my daughter so smitten." He leans back in his chair.

"I would just like to preface something though."

He gives me a pointed look. "Uh huh, and what's that?"

"He's a bit older than me."

"What's a bit?"

"He's younger than you!" I respond excitedly.

His eyes widen. "Raegan!"

I wince. "Forty-one?"

He blinks at me. "Excuse me? Forty—" He shoots to his feet. "You're twenty-two! NEWLY TWENTY-TWO! Like TODAY!" he shouts, although I know when Theo Graham is angry shouting and this isn't it. He takes a deep breath and I can tell he's arguing with himself. A flash of something I don't recognize crosses his face and it's almost as if he's conflicted. "I need to meet him."

"Yes!"

"Like today, young lady."

"Okay! But please be nice." I bite my bottom lip and look off to the side, as I prepare to tell the second most important guy in my life about the guy who recently dethroned him as the first. "I love him."

He narrows his eyes at me before he lets out a sigh. "Does he know that?" I nod. "Does he feel the same?" I nod again and he raises an eyebrow at me. "Did he say it first?"

Thoughts of the first time he said it a few days ago comes rushing back to me and I can't stop the smile from creeping onto my face.

I turn over, just as the last bit of sleep slips away one morning, and collide with Wes' hard body. I'm instantly comforted as his arms wrap around me. Heat floods me when I feel his dick pressing against me through his sweatpants. I press my face into his bare chest and sigh when I feel his lips on my head.

"I love you," I hear him whisper and my eyes shoot open.

My mouth drops open and tears flood my eyes because he said it. Oh my God!

I pull back immediately to look up at him, blinking away the tears. "You do?"

He stares at me, his eyes wide and then he clears his throat. "I did not think you were awake." He looks away from me and for the first time since he first expressed his feelings for me, I can see nerves all over his face. "I know it's soon—"

I turn his face to look at me. "Answer me."

"What do you think?"

"I think you do."

He smiles at me and I push him onto his back and straddle him. "I do." He nods. "I love you, Raegan."

"Oh my God." I press my lips to his. "I love you too."

"Yeah, Dad." I beam. "He said it first."

"Don't be nervous," I say as Wes and I stand outside my house. I'd gone outside when he got here to make sure he was okay before I brought him in.

"I'm not," he responds even as he pushes his glasses up his nose with his middle finger. *Something I notice he only does when he's anxious.*

"One, I was talking to myself, and two, you're a liar."

He narrows his gaze at me. "I'm meeting your father. It's a big deal. What do I do again?"

"You own a company! Just not the one I work for...get with the story!" I snap my fingers.

He chuckles. "Fine. If I say my last name, he won't put two and two together?"

"Oh, good call. He may not remember the company, but he might! My dad pays attention. Goddamn it. Okay, when I introduce you, I'm just not going to say your last name."

He tilts his head to the side. "Is that going to work?"

The door opens and my father stands in the entrance. "You guys just going to stand out here all day?" His eyes ping-pong back and forth between us.

"Dad, this is Wes!" I say about four octaves higher than my usual speaking voice and both of them look at me with amused expressions. I ignore their looks. "Wes, this is my father, Theo. You may know him from being in the NFL. Dad, Wes is a huge fan."

"I do appreciate the intro, as well as you trying to butter me up. Come on in," he says and we follow him in.

"Mr. Graham, it's very nice to meet you," Wes says, holding his hand out once we're in the foyer.

"Likewise. My daughter has had very nice things to say about you," my dad says as they shake hands.

The sounds of my sliding glass door opening and closing send me into a panic because Lucas wasn't supposed to be here!

"Dammit," I say under my breath.

"Well well well, what do we have here?" Lucas strolls into the room, pulling off a beanie and his coat.

"I thought you were going to the movies with Avery?" I say through gritted teeth.

"And miss out on meeting your boyfriend? Never. And I'm hurt that I wasn't included in this from the jump. HURT," he says and I glare at my dad who clearly must have told him about this. "I'm Lucas, Rae's very lovable—but will also kill for her—younger brother." He smiles and I glare at him with a look I hope he reads as *I'm going to kill YOU.*

"This is Wes," I grit out.

Wes chuckles next to me and shakes my brother's hand. "It's nice to meet you." I see him looking at me in my periphery before he turns back to Lucas. "I know it seems like she's not too happy with you right now, but she's crazy about you. Both of you really. It's a little intimidating to meet the only two men that have ever meant anything to her." My heart softens and I'm immediately less irritated with Lucas. I look up at him before shooting my eyes to my brother and father.

"Damn," Lucas says as he looks to my father. "I kind of like him." He rubs his jaw. "What was I supposed to say again? Oh! The age thing." He looks back to Wes. "You're kind of old for Rae, what's that about?"

"Lucas!" I stomp my foot at him.

"What?!" He shrugs. "It's a valid question. Also, I do actually have plans with Avery, so can we wrap this up?" He spins his index finger in a circle.

"You're not helping. Go away." My dad's eyes snap to Lucas.

"I'm just messing with you," Lucas says with a slap to Wes' back. "Not about the killing for her thing though." He points a finger at him. "Remember that."

The rest of the interaction goes fine, albeit a little awkward, and the three of us—*against my will*—are supposed to have dinner next week.

We are at dinner in a private room of one of my favorite restaurants having just finished the best crème brûlée I've ever had when Wes moves back from the table and pats his lap. I'm out of my chair instantly, like that simple gesture is a call my body can't resist. I'm in his lap and he trails a finger over my face. "Happy birthday, beautiful."

"Thank you."

"I have something else for you."

"If it's another *Cartier* box, you're returning it."

He rolls his eyes followed by a look that lets me know he's planning to test that in the near future. He hands me an envelope and the first thing I notice when I open it, is the words are not in English. "It's in French."

"You can't read it? Did you lie in your interview?" His mouth drops open as he tuts at me.

I glare at him before reading that we have dinner reservations at *Le Cinq* for Valentine's Day weekend next month.

"Are you telling me we are going to Paris for Valentine's Day?"

He squints his eyes at the paper. "Is that what it says? My French isn't great."

"Wes…" I set the paper down and push my lips to his. "I love you so much." *And Christ, do I.* "Does this mean we can go shopping too?"

"Only if I can come with you in the dressing room again."

"Absolutely." I tell him. We kiss for I don't know how long before he pulls away.

"You know, I've been thinking about something you said a month ago." I narrow my eyes wanting him to go on. "About why I'm not married." I nod, remembering. "I figured out why." I run my fingers through his hair as I wait for his response. "So, I'd be available when you were ready for a husband."

Epilogue

Raegan

May 2023

OH. MY. GOD.

See what happens when you don't use condoms?

I'm honestly surprised this didn't happen sooner.

Remember all those times you guys were fucking with no protection in the beginning? You're lucky your "pull and pray" method worked this long.

You're pregnant!

Oh my God. Wes is going to freak.

Yeah, be freaking ecstatic.

He's been trying to knock you up for months.

No wonder, I've felt like such shit these last few weeks.

And that aversion to fucking everything?

And my boobs. I think about that night Wes nibbled on them and I almost cried because they were that sensitive.

These are all the thoughts I have while I'm staring at the three pregnancy tests in my hand, a smile pulling at my lips as I think about having a baby with the love of my life.

I bounce on the balls of my feet just as I hear his voice from the bedroom.

"Baby, are you ready to go?"

"Just a sec!" I yell through the door.

Most days we do go in to work together after the entire office was made aware that we are in a relationship. Surprisingly, no one really cared. Except for Liam, who not so surprisingly no longer works for the company. There were a few catty and snide comments that Wes rectified immediately and thoroughly explained what would happen if *anyone* had anything to say regarding our private life.

On that note, we do try to remain as professional at work as possible. I'm no longer his assistant and don't report directly to him, and while we do have lunch together most days and there have been many quickies in his car, it is *very rare* that we fool around in the *Beckham Securities* offices.

Especially once I moved in with him where he had access to me all the time; it tempered our obsession with each other.

Sort of.

I know I can't wait the whole day without telling him, but this is just so anticlimactic. *Should I plan a cute reveal?* I clean the tests off, toss them in my purse, and open the door. He smiles at me as he slides his jacket on. "You're so beautiful." He crosses the room. "Every time I look at you, you take my breath away."

My heart flutters in my chest, just like it always does whenever this man opens his mouth. "Wes."

"Oh, before I forget I do have to go to New York Friday for a meeting and I'll be back early evening so I'm going to be a little late for Avery's graduation party. I'm sorry. I'm going to come straight from the train."

I shake my head, not wanting him to worry about that. "Oh baby, it's okay. You don't even have to come."

"Of course, I do. She's important to you and your family," he says before he pecks my lips. "You ready to go?"

"Wait, I want to tell you something because if I don't it's going to burst out of me."

WES

Those blue eyes that have such a sharp grip on my heart look up at me, and I can't escape the way I feel when she looks at me this way. I have an inkling of what she's dancing around because I know Raegan Graham better than I know how to run my company—*and I am not a billionaire by accident.*

"I'm pregnant." Those two words that I never thought I'd hear come out of my favorite person, and before I can speak, I've pressed my lips to hers. *Because holy shit, I'm going to be a father.*

And her husband because nothing can stop me now from using that ring I've had for three months.

"Raegan." When I pull back, tears have started to trickle down her face and I immediately begin wiping them. "We're going to have a baby?" She nods, the tears flowing faster now. "It's about time," I chuckle, trying to keep my own tears at bay. "I am so fucking happy."

"Me too." Then, she's in my arms, her legs wrapped around my waist as she presses her lips to mine again.

Raegan

Three Months Later

"I never would have pegged you for a shotgun wedding," Lucas says as he downs a glass of champagne, his third in the last ten minutes, and I wince.

I put my hands on my hips and glare at him. "It's not a shotgun wedding, and can you slow down? I am not rubbing your back while you puke at my own wedding."

"I'm sorry, are you pregnant or nah? Sounds like a shotgun wedding to me."

"Lucas…you're being a dick," I warn because although I know he's going through some shit, I'm not going to let him take it out on me on the biggest day of my life.

"Sorry." He sighs and my heart softens slightly knowing why he's in such a foul mood. I'm sure it's tough seeing the girl he spent years being in love with…dancing with *our dad.* I know he basically gave them his blessing but I know it's got to be tough.

"I'm so proud of you," I tell him. "I know that wasn't easy."

"What?" He snorts. "Oh yeah, it's fine." He waves it off, but I follow his gaze to Avery in her black bridesmaid dress being spun around the dance floor by my dad. "They love each other so…what can ya do?" He nods towards one of my bridesmaids who's moving towards the bar. "Your friend single?"

"I'm actually not sure. Maybe?"

"You mind?"

"If she's down, be my guest," I chuckle and he presses a kiss to my cheek before he moves through the crowd.

"Mrs. Beckham," I hear in my ear and when I turn around, I see my husband of the last few hours looking absolutely delicious in his tux. The tux he wore while we got married. *We are married and having a baby.* I beam at the thought because I truly don't think I've ever been this happy. "I think we are supposed to be attached at the hip tonight." He pulls me against him and rubs my ass. "I cannot wait to fuck my wife tonight," he whispers in my ear. "My pregnant wife. Jesus Christ, Raegan." He bites my neck and I yelp. "The second we are on that private jet, you're going to be naked for the entire flight to the Maldives."

"That's a long flight." I giggle.

"Not long enough for everything I want to do to you." He gives me a dangerously sexy look and there's a flutter between my legs.

"If I weren't already pregnant, something tells me I would be after this trip."

"Absolutely. I saw what you packed in your suitcase. We are going to be gone for two weeks and you only brought enough clothes for three days."

My mouth drops open. "You peeked! That lingerie was a surprise, Wesley!"

A guilty look crosses his face. "You left it open!"

"Besides," I smile innocently, "I didn't pack a bunch of clothes because I was kind of hoping we could make a little pit stop to go shopping." I hold my thumb and index finger very close together.

"Of course, baby. Where?"

"Dubai, again?"

"Okay." He chuckles as he pulls out his phone. "When were you going to tell me? Tomorrow when we were getting on the plane?" He chuckles. "You know a change in the flight plan requires longer than an hour's notice?"

"You can make it happen." I raise an eyebrow at him and he looks at me from over his glasses.

He pulls me into his arms. "Does it turn you on knowing the lengths I'll go to make you happy?"

"Yes."

He grins, revealing those dimples and I melt in his arms. "Are you wet right now knowing I'd do anything to see you smile at me the way you are?" He cups my face.

"Yes." I pull his face to mine and whisper against his lips. "Can we go to the bridal suite for a second?"

"Fuck yes. I've been dying to lick your pussy while you're wearing your wedding dress." Mischief crosses his face as he starts guiding me towards the exit when Avery comes over to us.

"It's time to throw the bouquet!"

"Now?" I ask as I look up at Wes. I bite my bottom lip.

"God, watching you two look at each other seems like I'm intruding on a personal moment." I turn back to Avery and I see the blush paint her tanned cheeks as she turns her head away from us. "I can come back?"

"No no," Wes starts. "Once I get her back there, I don't want anyone coming to look for her."

We make our way to the dance floor after they announce I'm tossing the bouquet. I turn around, keeping my back to the crowd before I send it soaring into the air behind me. I hear a bunch of women scream and then a squeal and when I turn around, I see Avery looking down at my bouquet in her hands. She looks up at me, somewhat panicked before a smile finds her face and I shoot her a wink.

"Shhh, there are people right outside my office door. They'll hear you, if you don't keep quiet," Wes says from between my legs, where his mouth has been for the better part of the last hour. We are on the jet, making use of the private bedroom doing our favorite role play which is mildly based on our life.

"Mr. Beckham," I moan out.

"Miss Graham." He licks through my slit. "You're so fucking wet."

"You make me so wet," I whimper.

"Will you let me fuck you here?"

"Yes."

"Can I come inside this sweet little pussy?"

"Yes."

He moves up my body, his naked form hovering above me. "Are you on the pill?" I shake my head and his nostrils flare. "So, I might get you pregnant?"

"Yes..."

"Fuck. Do you want that?"

"I...I don't know."

He swipes his dick through my pussy, rubbing the tip against my clit, and I feel that familiar metal against it. "Oh God, that feels good."

"You sure you don't know?"

"Yes, fuck me. I want it."

"If I get you pregnant, you might have to marry me." I giggle as he feeds me his cock, sliding inside of me slowly so I can feel each ridge of his dick.

"Okay."

He leans down and licks one of my nipples having learned

that biting is no longer a fun time for me. "You may have to fall in love with me too."

"Oh, how difficult for me."

He chuckles. "And be with me forever," he says as he begins thrusting.

I gasp, feeling myself build towards my climax already. "I can't wait."

The End.

Curious about Raegan's Dad, Theo and
the girl next door, Avery?

Check out

Prologue

Avery

THERE'S A SPIKE IN MY HEART RATE THE SECOND THEO Graham enters the room. My skin prickles and although I only notice him out of my periphery as my grandparents stand in front of me going on and on about how proud they are of me for graduating college, he has all of my attention.

Tonight is my graduation party and my parents rented out one of their favorite restaurants for the occasion and invited practically the entire town where I'm from in Pennsylvania to celebrate.

My back straightens as I follow him with my eyes, and suddenly I'm hyper-aware of everything. *How do I look? Is there anything in my teeth? Why are my hands sweaty? Has he noticed me? Fuck, Avery, do not look over there.*

Despite my instincts telling me not to react, I can't help it; my eyes are inexplicably drawn to Theo whenever we share a room. It's been like that for longer than I can remember. He knows how to command attention in any room. He knows how to command *my* attention anywhere.

God, he looks good.

At somewhere over six feet, Theo Graham is still *very* well built after his ten-year career in the NFL even though he now runs a construction company and is no stranger to getting his hands dirty. Warm chocolate brown eyes, a head full of lush dark brown wavy hair that is always styled perfectly, and a light dusting of stubble currently covering his jaw. There have been times he was clean-shaven and also times that he had a full beard so luscious it made me want to run my fingers through it.

Dressed in a linen charcoal gray suit with a black shirt that covers most of the delicious muscles I know are hiding beneath, he's making more than a few women's heads turn as he makes his way through the party.

I'm no stranger to witnessing the attention Theo gets, but it never stopped the sting of jealousy, especially now that I know what his mouth tastes like.

I want to kiss him again.

Two years before he retired from professional football and fresh off a divorce from the mother of his two children, Lucas and Raegan, the three of them moved into the house next door. I was only fifteen when he retired from the NFL, so I wasn't as familiar with the football star version of Theo. I knew the guy who ran four miles every day to stay in shape and worked out in his backyard which I had a perfect view of from my bedroom window. I knew him as the guy who picked Lucas and me up when we ran from a party that the cops busted, and to this day—*to my knowledge*—he'd kept that fact from my parents. I knew the man who helped teach me to drive while he was teaching Lucas because we were always attached at the hip.

Never did I think that he'd eventually be on the list of men

I'd go on to kiss in my lifetime. Especially when I'd spent the majority of my ninth-grade year making out with his son. *For practice, not for romance.*

I shiver thinking about that night when Theo had lifted me in the air and pressed me against the wall like I was nothing. Holding me up against him as he pressed his lips to mine. I can still recall that dizzy feeling of his hard body pressed against me and I feel my nipples harden and press against the fabric of my dark green dress at the memory.

I chose this color not only because it's the color of the tassels of my graduation gown but because it brings out the green in my eyes. My eyes typically dance between brown and hazel most of the time, but there are moments when the sun hits them just right when you can see flecks of green.

A fact that Theo had brought up on more than one occasion.

The dress is midi length, but hugs me in all the right places, highlighting my hourglass figure. I'm bronzed from my recent trip to the beach with my friends—our final girls' trip to commemorate the end of college and this chapter of our lives—and I can feel his gaze skating across me, heating the already warmed skin. *You would never know I had any melanin in me with how pale I can get during the winter months.* My hair, initially styled into perfect curls before the East Coast humidity got to it, has fallen into waves. I pull it over one shoulder to showcase my neck, which, if my memory serves me correctly, is Theo's weakness.

I catch his eyes again and he's closer than he was before, like he's making his way through the crowd to get to me.

I mean, it is my graduation party. It would be rude to not speak to the guest of honor.

My grandparents have moved on to mingle, leaving me alone holding a glass of champagne that I want to down before Theo gets to me. I try to meet his gaze again, waiting for him to approach me, and I realize that even though he's not looking at me I can sense that I have his attention.

I haven't seen Theo in almost six months. Six months ago, when we'd made out in his car and I'd sat in his lap and fucked myself with my fingers until I came with the promise of *more*.

It wasn't the first time we'd hooked up, having done so once the previous summer, but it was the furthest we'd ever gone. We hadn't spoken about it after, almost as if we were both pretending it hadn't happened. Me out of humiliation and hurt and him to keep it hidden from the one person he was sure it would hurt the most.

Lucas Graham.

My best friend.

His son.

Acknowledgements

Thank you so much for reading! I hope you loved reading about Wes and Raegan and if you've read *The Worst Kept Secret,* you loved being back with the Graham family! We'll be back again in 2024 with Lucas' book!

As always, it takes a village to deal with my chaos, so just a few thank yous!

Tanya, Rachel, Alexandra and Logan, thank you for everything. I'd seriously be lost without you guys! Thank you for being the best sounding boards and always being there. Love you guys so much!

Kristen Portillo, thank you for helping make this book perfect! One day I'll get my tenses and my timelines right the first time around. Until then, I'm grateful I have you to catch them. I appreciate you immensely!

Stacey Blake, thank you for always making the interiors so gorgeous and exactly what I want! Thank you for making my books so pretty!

Shaye and Lindsey, Thank you for all the things and keeping me so organized. What would I do without you? You guys are rockstars and I love you!

Ari Basulto, I would be lost without you. Thank you for all that you do to keep me organized! Thank you for running all of my teams and overall Q.B.'s life better than I could. A million thank yous.

Emily Wittig, thank you for another perfect cover! I think I say this every time, but this one may actually be my favorite! It's so pretty!

Pang Thao, thank you for all of my gorgeous teasers and

all of my last minute promo things and all the things I ask you to make me all the time. You're so good to me and I appreciate everything you do!

To the babes on my street team and ARC team, thank you for your excitement! Thank you for your love for me and my books and that you're always willing to let me take you over a cliff. The reason I can do what I do is because of you guys in my corner. Thank you for always clapping the loudest. I love you guys so big.

To all of the bloggers and bookstagrammers and TikTokers, thank you for your edits and your reels and your videos and always sharing my books! For still talking about books I wrote two and three years ago and loving them so much. For sharing with your friends (and sometimes your family? Ha) Thank you for everything you do. (Because seriously? Videos are so hard.)

And finally, and most importantly to YOU, to the readers, thank you for letting me into your minds and your hearts again with another book. I hope you enjoyed it! I love you all.

Also by Q.B. TYLER

STANDALONES

My Best Friend's Sister

Unconditional

Forget Me Not

Love Unexpected

Always Been You

What Was Meant to Be

Keep Her Safe

THE SECRETS UNIVERSE

The Worst Kept Secret

BITTERSWEET UNIVERSE

Bittersweet Surrender

Bittersweet Addiction

Bittersweet Love

CAMPUS TALES SERIES

First Semester

Second Semester

Spring Semester

Available through the Read Me Romance Audio Podcast

Fantasy with a Felon

About THE AUTHOR

Bestselling author and lover of forbidden romances, tacos, coffee, and wine. Q.B. Tyler gives readers sometimes angsty, sometimes emotional but always deliciously steamy romances featuring sassy heroines and the heroes that worship them. She's known for writing forbidden (and sometimes taboo) romances, so if that's your thing, you've come to the right place. When she's not writing, you can usually find her on Instagram (definitely procrastinating), shopping or at brunch.

Sign up for her newsletter to stay in touch!
https://view.flodesk.com/pages/6195b59a839eddd7aa02f8f

Qbtyler03@gmail.com

Facebook: Q.B. Tyler
Reader Group: Q.B.'s Hive
Instagram @qbtyler.author
Bookbub: Q.B. Tyler
Twitter: @qbtyler
Goodreads: Q.B. Tyler
Tik Tok: author.qbtyler

Made in the USA
Columbia, SC
07 December 2024

48665533R00140